Mitsurou Kubo

MOTEKI 2

Love Strikes!

c o n t e n t s

Moteki
Mitsurou
Kubo

chapter 16 ♥ Let's Meet With a Smile

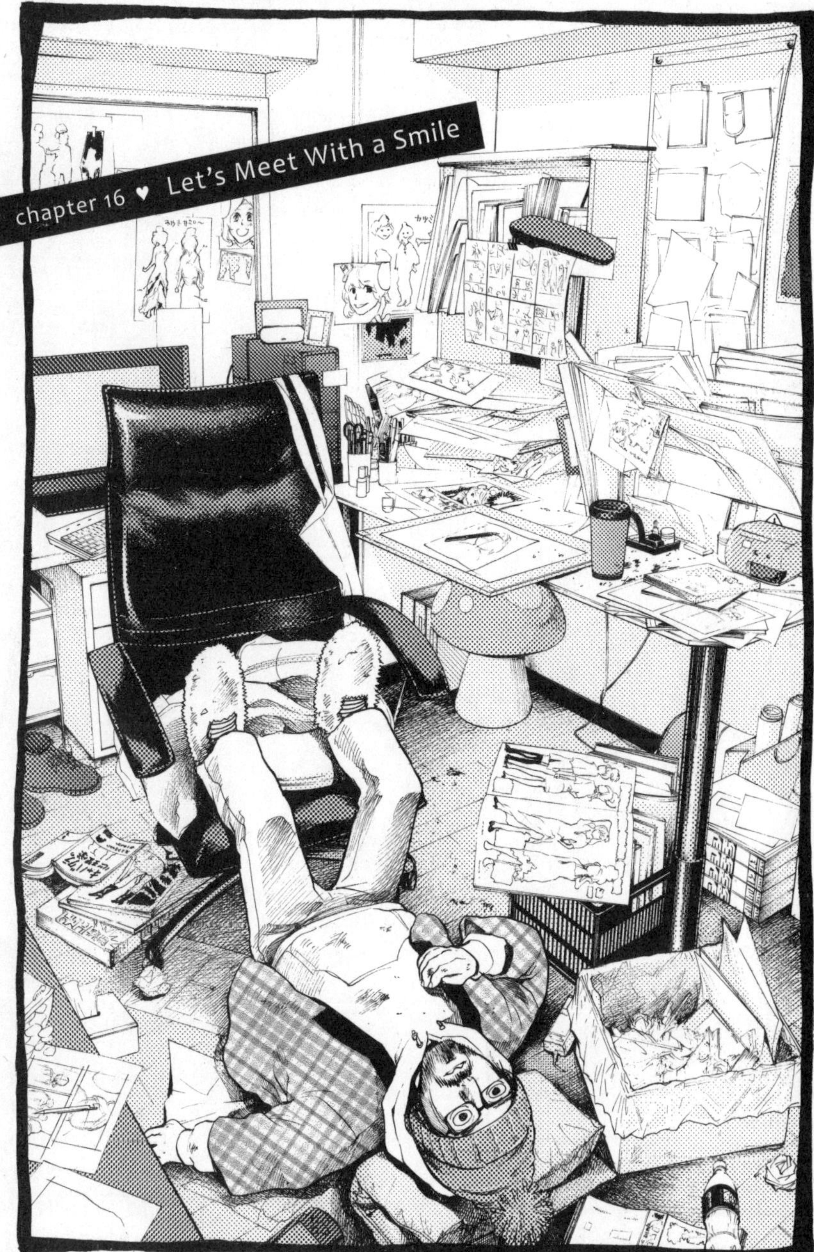

Omu-sensei ...
I put the leftover curry and rice in the fridge, so just micro-wave it if you want more.
Oh, and please be sure to open the Tupperware lid when you microwave it.
The tea and other stuff I bought online from Seiyu will show up tomorrow afternoon, so be ready for delivery.
Also ...
Well,
good luck on your manu-script !!

Uhm ...
SEN-SEI!
I'm well aware of how busy you are, but... could you... please sign this volume ?!
BAM

...
HRMF
NOOOOOO
Aah ...
You're working right now! Sorry!!

Well, sorry for the intrusion.
SNIFFLE
We'll be going now!

HUSSSH

KEEP IT UP, EVERYONE!!
Whoa !
O-Oh, sure, thanks.
Thank you.

BTAM

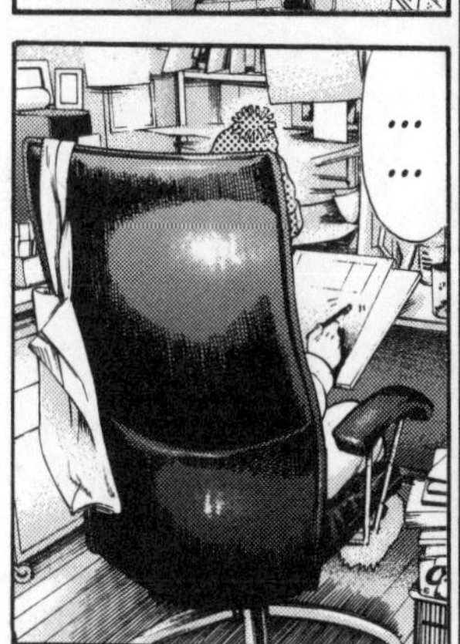
... ...

I wonder... if Omu-sensei hates me now...

You think so?

He never looked at me when he spoke to me...

I wasn't any use to him, either...

SNIFFLE SNIFFLE

Well, I was pretty pushy, myself.

But you're beautiful, Miss Doi, so he liked you.

GLOO OOOM

Must be nice...

I wish I was born beautiful.

If I'd been born as a beautiful woman,

I'd sleep with all sorts of men, one after another.

Then I'd marry the most talented one of the bunch, someone who makes money but is kinda dull, who seems like he wouldn't cheat...

I'd be his trophy wife, supporting him, having his kids...

Beauty genes mixed with genius genes would be tough to beat.

......

Man, that kind of life would be the best...

Uuuugh...
Huh? Did I say something weird just now?

Listen, Fujimoto.
Women aren't that wholly reliant on men when it comes to our own happiness.
Stop making assumptions like that.

Oh ...
Sorry ...
No, it's not like I'm mad or anything.

I mean, if I was you, I wonder if I'd be screwing tons of girls, one after another...
Wha? Not as a guy like me, you couldn't!

That's not true.
You're just not putting any effort into seducing women, right?
Be more confident!!

Well... I can't be confident ...
Most women would be totally creeped out if they knew about my life ...

No they would not!
They so would!
Why's that?
...

I'm 30 years old and have never had a girlfriend!
I've never had a woman tell me she loves me!
I've only had sex once in the past, and that was with a woman I didn't even like!
JOLT
How am I supposed to be confident when my life has been nothing but rejection?!
I don't have talent or money, I'm not even working toward anything.
HA HA
Women hate self-loathing guys like me, don't they?!
Why are you snapping at me?
If I'm a creep, then call me a creep! I already know I am!
I see...
So that's how it is.
GLOOOOOM
...
Is there anyone you like right now?
...
That girl in the photo?

She's ... well, just a friend ...
Any-one else?
Well, I believe there's someone out there under this vast sky.

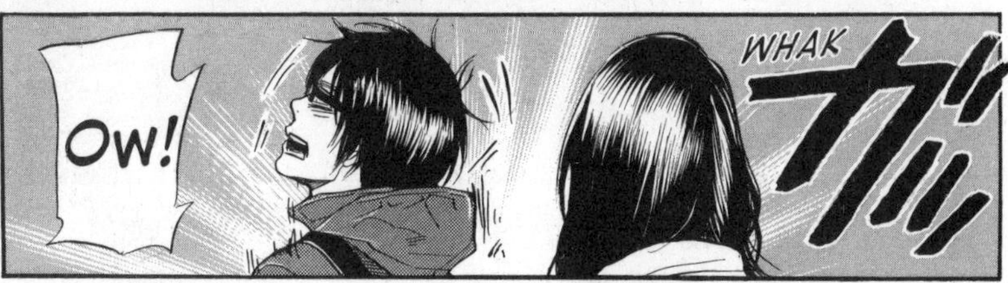
WHAK
Ow!

God, you piss me off!
Huh?
Wha?
That hurts!!
KICK
KICK
KICK
Stop acting like it's a done deal.
What are you, stupid?

MEDIA ARTS
OWL SPOT
E CA LYMPICS
OSHIMA PUBLIC
You know, Fuji-moto ...
I bet you wouldn't sleep with a girl unless she was on her hands and knees begging for it.
WHAT?!
Agh ...
I'm not *that* pas-sive ...

Are you sure ...?
HAH
Funny to hear that coming from you~!
Now she's suddenly acting all superior!!

Show me your hands.
BAM
YES'M !

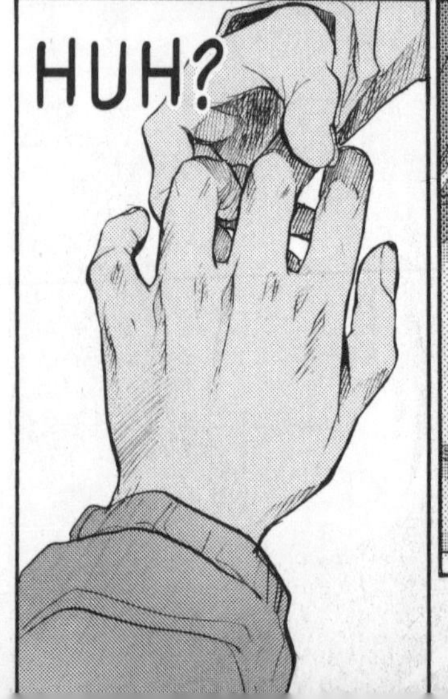
HUH?

TURN

Uhm... "Balse"?
Don't make me hit you.

Just to the train.
It's cold out.

I see. What a great idea!

Wow, it really is warm!

Isn't it?

WH—

WHAT'S GOING ON HERE?!

It's so deserted on Sunday nights even here in Ikebukuro, huh?
Yup ...
Back to work tomorrow...! I sure don't wanna go...
AAAGH!
WHAT A HOLLOW CONVERSA-TION!!
747
I'M PRETENDING TO STAY CALM WHILE WE TALK...
Me, too ...
BUT OUR HANDS ARE ALL OVER EACH OTHER DOWN THERE!
I need to be up early tomor-row.
Oof, for real ?
That is tough.
Yeah ...
So, I'm sorry, but ...
Oh, no, it's fine, it's fine.
I'M ACTING LIKE I UNDER-STAND WHAT'S GOING ON, BUT... WHAT IS THIS?!

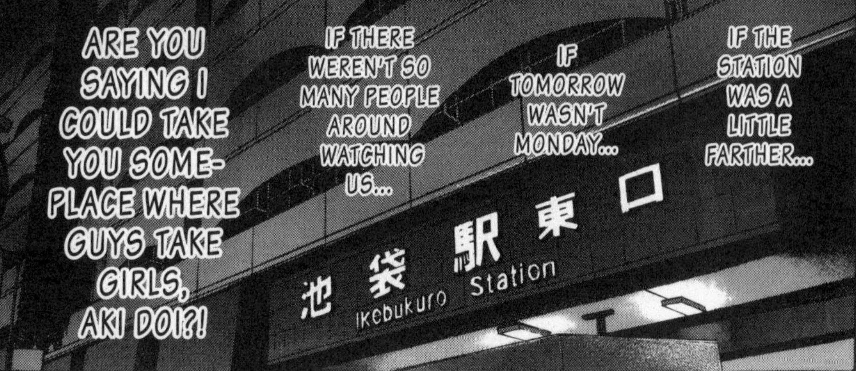

IF THE STATION WAS A LITTLE FARTHER...
IF TOMORROW WASN'T MONDAY...
IF THERE WEREN'T SO MANY PEOPLE AROUND WATCHING US...
ARE YOU SAYING I COULD TAKE YOU SOME-PLACE WHERE GUYS TAKE GIRLS, AKI DOI?!
池袋駅東口
Ikebukuro Station

Well.
Okay.
I'm this way.
Okay.
AH!

So ... let's do this again some-time.
Okay, yeah!
Maybe we can grab some-thing to eat some-place nice!

What about a hot pot at my place?
?!

Oh ...!
Yeah, sounds good!
I'll help make it!
I make a wicked chicken meat-ball hot pot!
Really?
You've gotta make it, then! Promise me, okay?!

Next time,
it's gonna be just the two of us, right?
O...
Of course...
ぎゅっ
GRIP

NEXT TIME WE MEET...

See, isn't the left one bigger?

wow, it really is!!

SOME-THING IS DEFINITELY GOING TO HAPPEN.

YOU CAN'T GET YOUR HOPES UP TOO MUCH. IT'S NEVER WORKED OUT FOR YOU BEFORE! WHY IS THAT CHANGING NOW?!

SHKK
SHKK

I'll call back again later.
Just so you know, we are behind schedule, so...
SHKK
BEEP
BEEP
SHKK

SHKK
SHKK
SHKK
SHKK
SHKK
SHKK
SHKK
SHKK

Hm hm hmm... Hm hm hm hmm ♬
SHKK
SHKK
SHKK

SHKK
SHKK
SHKK
MORE THAN A WEEK PASSED.
AND THEN

GLANCE
GLANCE
THAT GUY READING AN IDOL RUMOR MILL SITE.
THAT GUY PLAYING GAMES.
AND I'M TEXTING...
WITH A WOMAN!!

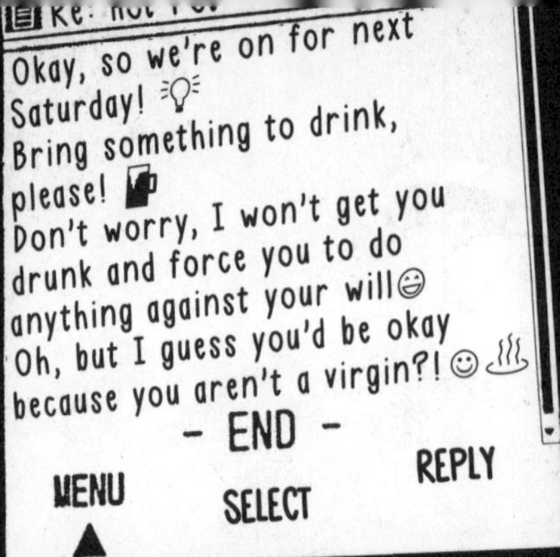

Okay, so we're on for next Saturday!
Bring something to drink, please!
Don't worry, I won't get you drunk and force you to do anything against your will
Oh, but I guess you'd be okay because you aren't a virgin?!

Re: Re: Hot Pot
I'm still an anal virgin so please be gentle with me...!!

WE'RE TRADING TEXTS THAT MAKE LIGHT OF OUR DIRTY FEELINGS WHILE STILL BEING SUGGESTIVE.

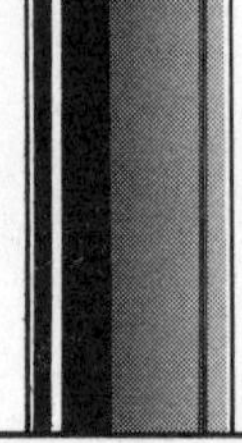

So not only are you passive, you're a bottom?! =3

Well, show up in your sexiest undies ♥
I'll give it my best, too!
(　￣□￣)

SMIRK
SMIRK
Aah ...
Damn you, Aki Doi...! Have you been specially trained in the art of making a man happy ?!
SMIRK

SHE'S BEAUTIFUL, KNOWS HOW TO COOK, AND CAN GET ALONG WITH ALL KINDS OF PEOPLE.
SHE'S PROBABLY BEEN IN REGULAR RELATIONSHIPS AND DONE A BUNCH OF SEX STUFF.
Men like
this kinda thing, right? I know, I know...
UNLIKE ME.

I HOPE SHE'S NOT GONNA MAKE FUN OF ME
IF I TAKE ALL OF THIS STUFF TOO SERIOUSLY.

My sense of inferiority is seeping into my desires!! Am I really gonna go to her place?
But ... Argh ...
Wait, is she trying to sell me something? Like a self-help seminar? A romance scam? Is she after something of mine?

THE HEAD HOSTESS IS 18?!
GET THIS PLACE BACK ON ITS FEET!!
I'M GONNA

GTUNG
GTUNG

Hey, Fuji! You see it?
AH HA HA
This week's Maga-zine!!

I am totally stun-ned!
Omu's new character has gotta be Doi.

Aki Doi won't get upset that
Omu drew this... will she?

I figured Omu was totally into her.
Thanks, Fuji!
MAGAZINE

So, I've got a request.
Can you ask Doi if she could start coming by to help as a part-time thing?
This is a shorter chapter than normal from him. I don't think he's quite stable yet.
And if Doi was there ...

MY IMAGINATION WENT INTO NEGATIVITY OVERDRIVE.

Huh?

No, I haven't read Magazine yet.

Oh, really?

I'll take a look soon.

Tell him I can help out.

Just weekends, right?

This week?
Uhm... In that case, he says he wants you to start this weekend.
Is that okay with you, Fuji-moto?
...
...

Uhm ... You're sure?
Yeah.
In fact, it's a help. I wanted to save up some money.

W-We can figure out another time.
Right?
Well.
Say hi to Omu-sensei for me.

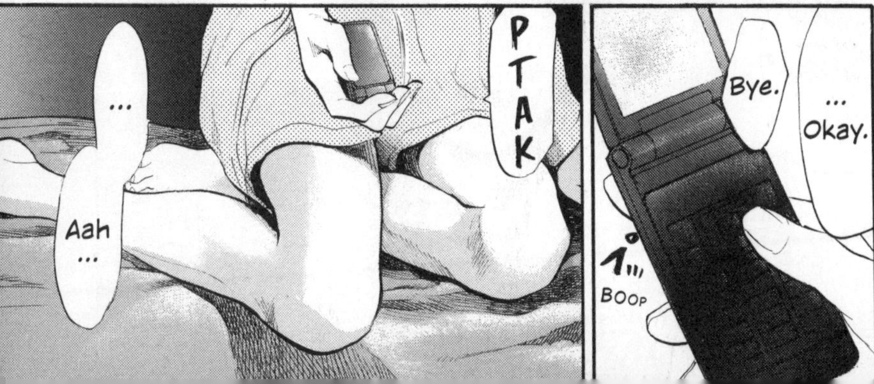
... Okay.
Bye.
BOOP
PTAK
...
Aah ...

THWAP
WHUMP

I FIGURED THERE'S NO WAY SHE'D EVER LOVE ME, SO I GAVE UP.

DING DOOONG

Ah!
Hello, there!

Huh?

Are you alone today, Sensei?

...

I'll start by cleaning up, if that's okay.

You just keep working, Sensei.

GACHAK

Ah!
Are you free right now, Fuji?
I was thinking of coming over with some souvenirs from Nagano.

Aah ...
Hm? Wait, were you asleep?
Yeah ... I'm fine. I didn't feel like moving ...
I bought a lot of things. There were a ton of cool places up in Ueda.
What do you want?
And I got some Sanada Yukimura goods!
Let's see, I have some *nozawana*, and wine, and wasabi seasoning ...

And jam.
MARMALADE
Do you like marma-lade?

BUT I STILL WANT TO KNOW.

ABOUT THAT DREAM
THAT WAS CUT SHORT LONG BEFORE YESTERDAY.
SPLSH
SPLSH
ZHAAA
...
Itsu-ka?
Yeah?
HSSSK
HSSSK
HSSSK
AH
I WANT TO KNOW WHAT HAPPENS TO US NEXT.

Sorry, I'm gonna help out, too!

Oh, and this is a friend.

Ah!

It's nice to meet you! I borrowed your manga from Fuji and I'm a huge fan now!

C-C-Could I get your auto-graph?!

Ah, the girl from the pic...

I'M PICKING AT THIS TRAUMA FOR AS LONG AS I CAN!!

... ...

Oh, and these are souvenirs from Nagano! Please take them!

chapter 16 ♥ END

chapter 17 ♥ Swimming

"WOMEN HATE BEING COMPARED."
I KNOW THAT LINE FROM A KYOKO FUKADA SONG, BUT THAT'S EXACTLY THE CRIME I'M TRYING TO COMMIT RIGHT NOW.

Nice to meet you.

My name's Aki Doi, I'm helping out here starting today.

Aki Doi (27), office temp.

Born in Chiba. Boyfriend-less for 1.5 years.

Oh!

I'm Itsuka Naka-shiba.

Sorry to both-er you!

Itsuka Nakashiba (23), lighting assistant.

Born in Kanagawa. Boyfriend-less for her entire life.

YOU LITTLE HOME-WRECKER...!
SLEEPING WITH ANOTHER WOMAN'S MAN?!
SHUT UP, YOU OLD HAG!
FUCK OFF!
...THIS KIND OF SCENE...

WON'T HAPPEN. I HAVEN'T GONE OUT WITH EITHER OF THEM LONG ENOUGH FOR THIS TO TURN INTO A BLOODBATH.
I'D LIKE TO GO OUT WITH ONE OF THEM SOMEDAY, BUT I STILL CAN'T DECIDE WHICH.

...
Oh, Omu-sensei!
If there's anything I can help with, just let me know!!
プイッ
HMF
Did we make him mad...?
Uh...

I'm so glad you two showed up!
Could you help with cleaning, or maybe airing out the futon?
Roger Wilco, over and out!!
Excuse me for a second.
Let's hang this thing up!
SHAKK
...

C'mon ...!
BAM
Why did he just show up out of nowhere ?!
SWIPE
SWIPE
I barely put any effort into my makeup because I thought I'd only be seeing Omu-sensei today!
KSST
KSST
I wore totally unfeminine clothes because I thought they'd get filthy from cleaning!

And of all the times ...
why would he bring that girl here ?!

I DON'T UNDERSTAND WHAT MAKES HIM THINK HE CAN WALTZ IN HERE AFTER BREAKING HIS PROMISE TO COME OVER TO MY PLACE, EITHER!
SNAP
THE HELL IS HE THINKING ?!

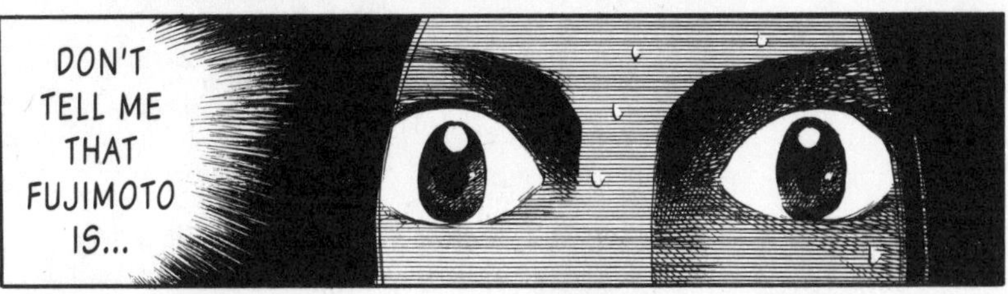

DON'T TELL ME THAT FUJIMOTO IS...

Y'know, Miss Doi, I think you like me or some-thing ...

but I'm already going out with this chick, actually.

Sorry!

It was just hard to say something, y'know? Real sorry if I made you feel something for me.

Holding your hand and all... (lol)

You're a real sexy thing, huh? (lol)

Can't you figure this out without me having to tell you?

FUJI

Oh, so she's just some boring old lady?

Wow, she must be desperate to find a man at her age ...

TOILET
You've got the wrong idea! It's not like I've gone head-over-heels chasing after you!!
I don't like you *that* much, you dumb-ass!
BAM
BAM
BAM
Miss Aki is really pretty.
I bet guys love her!!
WHAP
I forget, is she dating Omu-sensei?
Huh?!
No way.
We only just met Omu-sensei the other day!!
WHAP
WHAP

I didn't think I'd ever come back to this building ...
Ah!
This is where Mr. Sumi brought me...

I'm fine now, I wouldn't mind seeing him. And I wanted to meet Omu-sensei, too.
For real?

NEVER IN MY LIFE HAVE I BEEN THE ONE TO TELL SOMEONE I LIKED THEM.
IT'S ALWAYS BEEN SOMEONE ELSE TELLING ME, OR ME MAKING THEM SAY SO.

Were you okay with curry again, Omu-sensei?

Eat up, okay?
This is yummy!
Oh, is it?
?!
MNCH
MNCH

This is so good!
It's super tasty, Miss Aki!

You're such an amazing woman, Miss Aki! I wanna be like you!
ぱくっ
SHOVEL
I can't cook at all... I can't do anything girly, really...
ぱくぱくっ
SHOVEL

Thank you.
You're still young, Itsuka. And you're cute!!
You've got great skin, too.
Whaaaa?
No way, that is not true at all!
NO WAY
Men just love women like you, Miss Aki!!

Right, Fuji?
Huh?
Uh, yup.

Re-ally?
You'd prefer some-one younger, right, Fuji-moto?

Huh?

Y'know, you two look like love-birds, the way you're both wearing stripes. (lol)
Ah!
No, this was by chance...

Oh, so you two are dating after all?
You should've told me, Fuji-moto...! Geez!
No!
Ah...
It's not like we're going out...
SIGH
Don't say that, think of the poor girl's feelings...

Do you not have a boy-friend, Miss Aki?
Nope, I don't ...
Know anyone good ?

Eh, there's no one around me who'd make a good boy-friend.
They're either dirt poor or married, or...
What's your type?
Hmm...
I wouldn't say I have any strict require-ments, but...

Someone with career goals would be nice.
Someone who can take action and expects a lot of himself ...
Yeah, instead of being all talk !!
More than anything, I just want someone I can respect.
Oh, I totally get that!!
...
Right on!!

Oh, I'm not trying to bash on you or anything, Fujimoto. Don't mind me.
You've got your own good points.
AT LEAST SAY IT LIKE YOU MEAN IT!!

I don't have a good job, I don't have any dreams, and I don't have any money.

And thanks to that, not a single girl is interested in me!

Next time,

ARE YOU GOING TO LET YOUR SELF-LOATHING

What about a hot pot at my place?

I'm just ...

WHAT'S GOING ON HERE?!

Stop acting like it's a done deal.

What are you, stupid?

ERASE EVERY SINGLE THING THAT I DID?!

WHAT A HOLLOW CONVERSATION!

Uhm ...

MUTTER

You know, I want to change ...

But it's like a chicken and egg problem, and...

MUTTER

Seconds ...

DO YOU HAVE ANY IDEA

Oh!

JUST HOW MUCH I'VE PUT INTO THIS?!

Omu-sensei. Don't you like women like Miss Aki?

AH!

...

"Go ahead, but your lips just! Might! Get! Burned!!"
WHPP
Huh?
Aah ha ha! There it is! The catchphrase that Donald, the handsome, bad-boy host uses in "The Head Hostess is 18?!" !!

...

Ah ha ha ha ha! You're so funny, Omu-sensei!
Oh, so you sometimes make jokes, too!
Sorry, I haven't really read it all...
MEN ARE HARD FOR ME TO DEAL WITH BECAUSE THEY'RE EASIER TO HURT THAN I THOUGHT.

UNTIL NOW, MEN ALWAYS HAD THEIR OWN EXPECTATIONS OF ME, AND THEY'D GET DISAPPOINTED IN ME ON THEIR OWN.
IT WAS ALWAYS THE GUY WHO SAID WE SHOULD BREAK UP.

THAT'S WHY PEOPLE STARTED TO SEE ME AS A CONFIDENT WOMAN.

BUT I'M NOT CONFIDENT IN MYSELF EITHER, YOU KNOW?
ARE YOU NOT GOING TO NOTICE UNLESS I TELL YOU?

Okay, I'm gonna take the trash out.
Thank you!

WEEEEM!!

Huh...
Do I really have the right to be the one choosing between those two?!
Conveniently believes that he's unable to hurt someone else's feelings because he has such a low opinion of himself.

GSHK
GSHK
GSHK
GSHK
Me? Someone who's only ever known rejection?!
Even though I'm the real trash here?!

IT'S SUPER EASY BEING WITH ITSUKA.
SHE KNOWS WHO I AM WHEN I'M BEING MYSELF. I DON'T HAVE TO BE ON MY TOES WITH HER.
BUT WHEN I'M WITH AKI DOI, I SHOW OFF ONE MINUTE AND ACT PITIFUL THE NEXT.
I FEEL SO UNCERTAIN AROUND HER BECAUSE IT'S LIKE SHE'S TESTING ME.

SO...

IN THAT CASE, WHO DO I LIKE MORE?

I'm back!

Hm? Where's Miss Doi?

Huh?

She just left. You didn't run into her?

Heh... Just as long as Sumi doesn't try to hit on her or something...!!
I'm sure she'll be right back!

She made too much curry so she took some to Mr. Sumi's office.
HUH ?!

30 MINUTES LATER ...
I'm gonna go check !!
The 6th floor !

THAT CREEP IS CAPABLE OF ANY-THING!!
It's true. Women who are good at making curry are good at making love...
I can't believe the way men say that kinda thing... Silly!

BANG
BANG
BANG
BANG
MISS DOI ?!
MISS DOI ?!

What do you want? Keep it down !
GA
?!
CHAK

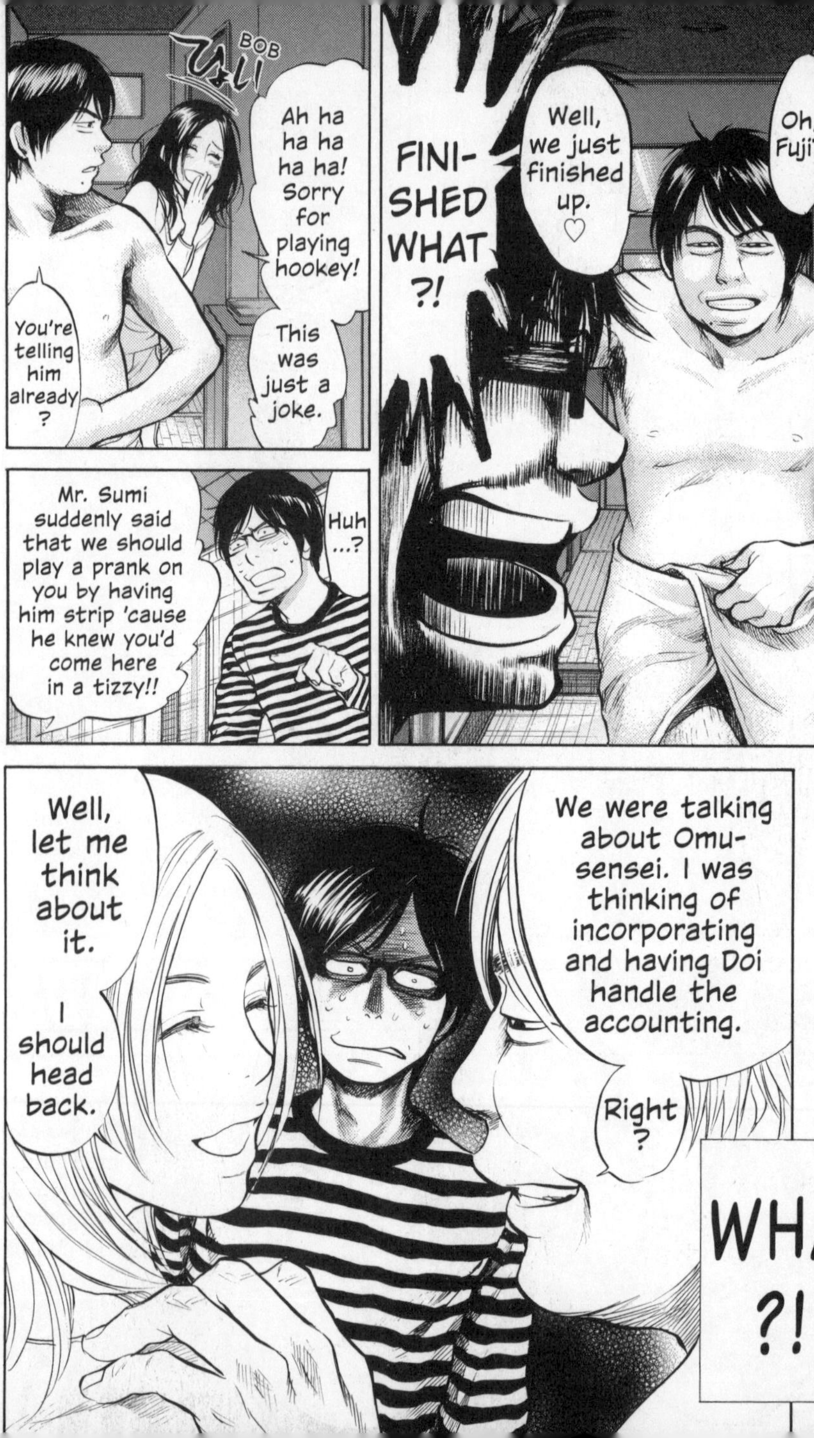

Oh, Fuji?

Well, we just finished up. ♡

FINI-SHED WHAT ?!

ひょい BOB

Ah ha ha ha ha ha! Sorry for playing hookey!

This was just a joke.

You're telling him already ?

Huh ...?

Mr. Sumi suddenly said that we should play a prank on you by having him strip 'cause he knew you'd come here in a tizzy!!

We were talking about Omu-sensei. I was thinking of incorporating and having Doi handle the accounting.

Right ?

Well, let me think about it.

I should head back.

WHA ?!

Fuji-moto?
What's wrong?

Hey, Fuji-moto!
...

You know, Miss Doi, I've always thought...
Don't you think you pander to guys a little too much?

You're gonna give men the wrong idea doing that.
What if some weirdo starts to take that seriously?

Wha ?
That's not what I was trying to ...
You need to be more aware of how beautiful you are. Guys are idiots, so they'll try and pull something if you're nice!
Don't act kind to men if you can't deal with the consequences.
We'll only get hurt with that half-assed sympathy of yours.

If there's something you want to tell me, just say it already.
I am super pissed off about the way you've been acting today, Fujimoto.
...
Well ...!
There's something I always wanted to ask you, too!

Miss Doi.

Are you in love with me?

HUSSSH
WAIT, SHE WENT QUIET ?!
Of course I'm not! Don't get so carried away, you idiot! You've never been more than eraser scraps to me!
IMAGINED SCENARIO
In that case, stop being so nice to me, you dumb-ass!
...IS WHAT I EXPECTED TO HAPPEN, BUT...
Uhm...
...
HELLOOOO...?
I do not want to say it.

LOOK AT THAT...
AKI DOI, YOU REALLY ARE ADORABLE.

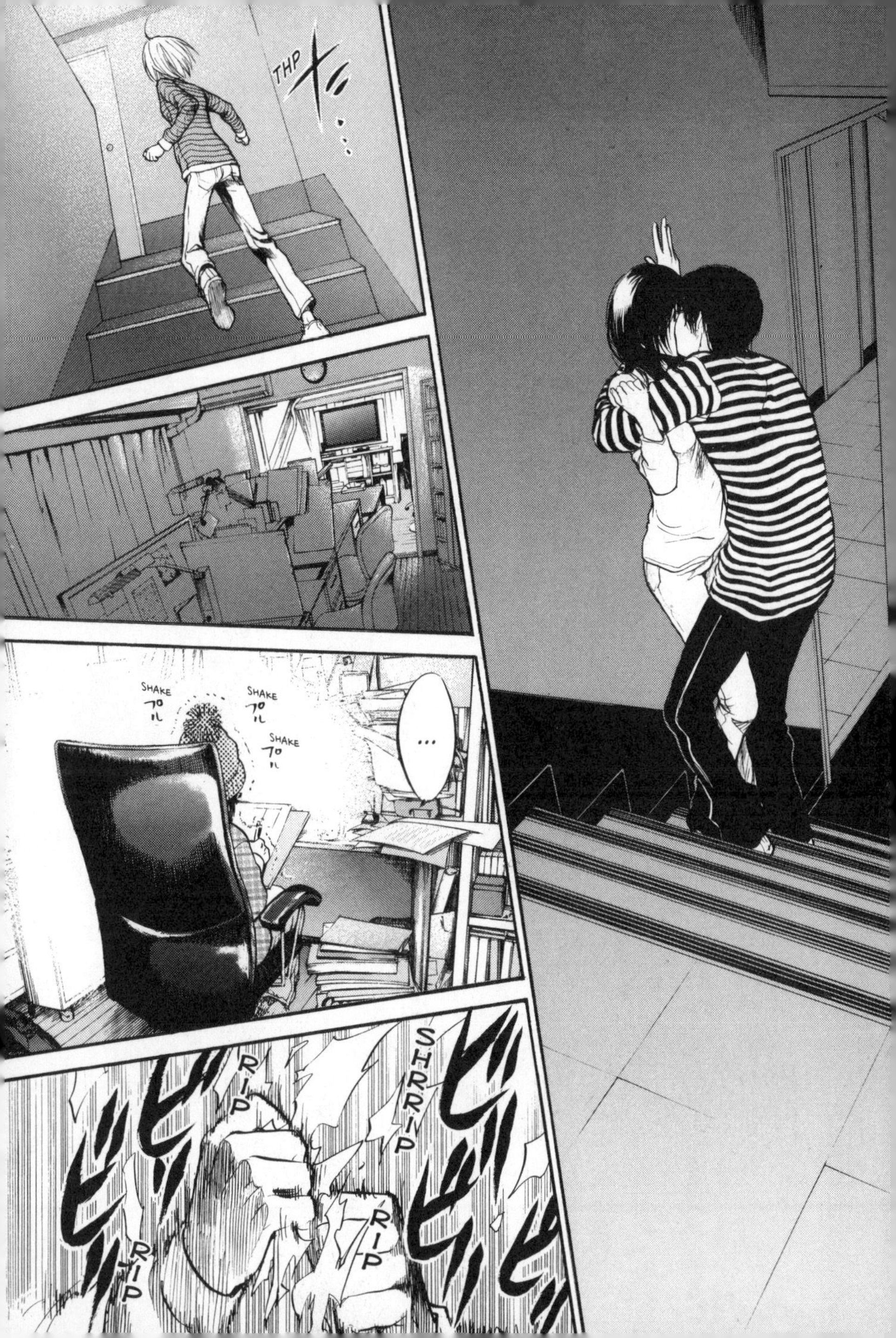
THP
SHAKE
SHAKE
SHAKE
...
SHRRIP
RIP
RIP
RIP

None of them really give a damn about my manga, do they?!

How can I get any work done when I'm this distracted?!

I'm so jealous I feel like I'm gonna die! Death by envy!

Yukiyo Fujimoto... How dare you make Aki Doi suffer like that in front of me...
I'll never for-give you ...!

chapter 17 ♥ END

chapter 18 ♥ The Eternal Puzzle

LET'S SAY

THAT I HAD A CHOICE BETWEEN TWO LIVES.

Mh ...

...

A LIFE WHERE I CAN KISS AKI DOI...

AND A LIFE WHERE I CAN'T KISS AKI DOI. WHICH WOULD I PICK?!

ISN'T IT OBVIOUS?

OF COURSE THE LIFE WHERE I CAN KISS AKI DOI IS BETTER!!

MY MOTEKI STARTED WITH THAT MESSAGE FROM HER.
WHILE I'VE HIT SOME SLUMPS...

I'VE BEEN ABLE TO KISS EVERY ONE OF THESE WOMEN!

AND NOW...
Mm.
Hey ...
C' mon.
THE DOOR TO AKI DOI HAS OPENED!
(AT LEAST, I THINK IT HAS...)

I GUESS IT'S MORE LIKE I'M FINALLY ABLE TO WALK THROUGH THE DOOR.
ARGH! I SHOULD'VE JUST BURST THROUGH IT SOONER!!
THIS IS THE BEST!!
BAM
Fuji-moto !!

Hm ...? What ?
Huh ?
It's not fair ...
What isn't ?

What's going on between you and Itsuka?

... ...

Something big enough to make you clam up.
No!
We haven't done it, really!
We haven't gone that far! I'm serious!

But you got close to going all the way.
...
You don't need to stay silent.
I'm not gonna get mad or something.

What's going on between you and Itsuka right now?
I want you to be honest. Tell me the truth.

Uhm ...
Well ...

Itsuka and I are ...
JOLT
BATAM

Oh ...
Sorry about the fuss.
Thanks for having me.
I'll be leaving now.

WHAT WAS THAT JUST NOW...?

FUJI WAS THE ONE...

GOING IN FOR A KISS WITH MISS AKI.

Itsuki, I still don't really know whether I'm in love with you or not.
I COULDN'T STOP THINKING ABOUT SOMETHING WHEN I SAW HER.
IT SEEMED LIKE SHE THOUGHT OF FUJI AS MORE THAN JUST A GUY FRIEND.
AND AFTER EVERYTHING HE SAID TO ME...
I'M SUCH AN IDIOT FOR BELIEVING HIM!
After that,
will you think about me one more time?
WHOA!
BAMM
You're so cruel, Fuji!

Tch.
...What the hell?!
Ah!
I'm sorry.
Ike-bukuro is scary...
?!

BEAUTIES

I'M AN IDIOT.

Yes, I just finished!

Uh-huh, I'm heading back now. ♡

Here's the place! ♡

ASSAGE PARLOR
DVD
40 MINS
4000 YEN
PEACH BEACH
I'D THOUGHT THAT FUJI WAS SO UNPOPULAR WITH WOMEN
THAT I WAS SAFE, THAT HE WOULDN'T RUN OFF TO ANYONE ELSE.
I'D LOOKED DOWN ON HIM, ASSUMING THAT SOMEONE WITH SO LITTLE CONFIDENCE COULD NEVER SEDUCE A BEAUTIFUL WOMAN.
2F

LOVE
LOOK
BUT I WAS WRONG.
HE DOESN'T GO AFTER WOMEN ON HIS LEVEL.
AND IT'S BECAUSE HE HAS SO LITTLE CONFIDENCE IN HIMSELF
THAT THERE'S A HOLE IN HIM THAT ONLY SOMEONE BEAUTIFUL CAN FILL.

And well, anyway...
that's... how Itsuka and I turned out to be kind of more than friends but not quite lovers...
I... still don't really know if I love her or not... And it's not like we're dating, but... uhm...

Sorry...

Ugh...
JOLT

...

KLOP
KLOP
KLOP
KLOP

I get it.
Any-way, let's get back to work.
Omu-sensei's been all on his own this whole time.

PAH
?!

Itsuka's such a nice girl.
I could tell by her face that she trusts you.
Are you going to betray her?
... ...
GRR
I don't have a clue what you're thinking right now, Fujimoto.
I feel like an idiot for letting you lead me on.
Do I have to set everything up for you to make a single move?
OH...
Soo ...
Back then, Yukiyo ...
I've thought this for a while about you, Fujimoto, but...

WHY DO YOU GET THAT WAY WHEN I SAY ONE LITTLE THING?
ONCE AGAIN,
STOP LOOKING SO SCARED, I JUST...
...
YOU KNOW, TODAY WE WERE SUPPOSED TO GO TO MY PLACE
SO WHY WOULD YOU BRING THAT GIRL HERE? I DON'T GET IT, WHY?!
IT'S ALL MY FAULT.
DOM
DOM
RETREAT!
Hurry, Retreat!
Retreat before we get killed!
RUN!

...Huh?
What's that?
Snapping at me again?
All of it was my fault.

I promise I won't do this kind of thing again.
I'm truly sorry for causing you all this trouble and making you feel so awful.

HUH...?

DON'T TELL ME...

IS THAT ALL IT TAKES TO MAKE HIM SEAL HIMSELF AWAY?

What a pain in the ass...
I'll just ignore him for a bit ...
Sorry for being late!

SLUURCH
...

Uhm ...
Huh ?
Where did Itsuka go?
VVT VVT VVT VVT

Hold on, did she already leave?
Omu-sen-sei?
NOD
I wonder if some-thing happened ?
What do you think, Fujimoto ?
Oh, you're still shutting yourself away.

ITSUKA

Sorry, I saw you guys kissing.
You can just ignore me now, it's fine. You don't need to contact me. Just do whatever you want.
- END -

MENU
SELECT
REPLY

Fuji-moto?!
I SHOULDN'T REACH FOR ANYTHING MORE.
I SHOULDN'T BE HERE.
GETTING INVOLVED WITH SOMEONE MEANS BRINGING TROUBLE INTO THEIR LIFE.
Lis-ten...
It's not like I'm that mad at you, so could you at least reply?

...WAIT, NO!!
I'M SINKING INTO THE SAME ALL-OUT SELF-FLAGELLATING MINDSET THAT I NEARLY ALWAYS FIND MYSELF IN WHENEVER SOMEONE GETS MAD AT ME!
PAPAPAPAM
WHENEVER ANYONE HURTS ME, I JUST DIG DEEPER INTO THOSE WOUNDS, LOOKING AT THEM LIKE, "THIS IS WHAT YOU WANTED, RIGHT?" WHY DO I LASH OUT LIKE THAT?
Zip
Zip
Zip
PAPAM

I'M 30 NOW. I GET IT.
I'M ONLY HURTING THEM, NOT MYSELF.
I MADE ITSUKA FEEL AWFUL.
I'VE BEEN NOTHING BUT RUDE TO AKI DOI, TOO.
Ahh!?

I NEED TO THINK ABOUT WHAT I'VE DONE, APOLOGIZE, AND ASK FOR FORGIVENESS.

I HAVE TO EARNESTLY CONTROL MYSELF AND PUT REAL EFFORT INTO BECOMING MY IDEAL SELF AS FAST AS POSSIBLE. I WANT TO BE A SOCIALLY UPSTANDING, BROAD-MINDED ADULT MAN WHO'S KIND TO THOSE AROUND HIM.

YEAH, THAT'S RIGHT.
I NEED TO THINK OF OTHERS BEFORE MYSELF.

I KNOW THAT.
Omu-sensei!!
P...
Please, will you shake hands with me?!
?!
...
When I read your manga,
it made me want to do my best and get to work.
I NEED TO BE THE ONE FALLING IN LOVE WITH OTHERS.
I COMPLETELY UNDERSTAND THAT.
I love your manga, Omu-sensei.

...
You'll always have my support!!
I WON'T BE ABLE TO DO A THING UNLESS I'M CONFIDENT IN MY OWN EMOTIONS.

Where did that come from...
Fujimoto?
Sorry to bother you.

I WANT TO BE LOVED DESPITE HAVING NO SELF-CONFIDENCE.

BUT WHEN I DO MEET A WOMAN WHO'S KIND TO ME, THEN I START SEARCHING FOR PROOF THAT SHE DOESN'T LOVE ME.

SINCE I DON'T LOVE HER YET, ALL I FOCUS ON IS WHETHER OR NOT I'M DOING ENOUGH TO GET HER TO LOVE ME.

I FEEL UNSURE BECAUSE I DON'T KNOW WHAT WOULD MAKE HER LOVE ME.
I DON'T KNOW WHO I SHOULD BE.

I CAN ONLY IMAGINE HOW MANY MORE TIMES SHE'LL BE FLABBERGASTED BY ME AND ABANDON ME IF I KEEP SEEING HER.
Hey, are you listening to me?
I DON'T FEEL ANY LOVE FOR HER,
WHICH IS WHY IT'S SO EASY FOR ME TO RUN AT THE MOST IMPORTANT TIMES.

I'm never going to do anything like that again.
And I'm not going to see Itsuka anymore, either.
What?!
Then what's your plan?!
Good-bye!
BAM
I'D RATHER SPEND MY WHOLE LIFE UNABLE TO LOVE.
Hey...
Fuji-moto!
Listen when people are trying to talk to you!!
AHHHhhh!
I'LL NEVER LOVE ANYONE.
THAT'S WHAT I'LL DO.

BTAM
Wait... What?!
Don't tell me his plan is to never open up...
WOBBLE
After all of these negotiations? What am I supposed to do with my feelings now...?

I CAN'T BELIEVE HE'S THAT FRAGILE...
...
WHAT ON EARTH HAS TRAUMATIZED YOU THAT BADLY?!
OPEN UP THOSE BORDERS!!

Miss Doi.
BADUM
Oh! Yes?
I'm sorry about the ruckus.

Wait... Was that the first time he's ever used my name?
What is it, Omu-sensei?
...

I need to draw hostesses in regular street clothes...
and I was wondering what would be good...
Huh...
I don't have a clue, so...
LadyLike
Will THIS attract guys?!

...
Something like this... And if you're going to add accessories, big ones would be good.
Oh, but a girl who likes designer brands might like this instead...
For shoes...
FIDGET
もじ
I... I wanted to buy some for reference...
It's hard to tell what they look like just with photos...
I always wanted to buy them... but it's hard for me to go to these stores, and... uhm...
FIDGET
もじ
NOD
In that case,
do you want me to go shopping with you?
FEND
IT'LL PROBABLY BE BETTER FOR EVERYONE
IF I STAY OUT OF THEIR LIVES.

NO. NO, I CAN'T KEEP THINKING THIS WAY!
DIDN'T I DECLARE THAT I'D CHANGE?!
RUNNING AWAY NOW IS THE SAME THING I'VE ALWAYS DONE!
WASN'T I GOING TO TACKLE THIS HEAD-ON?! BUT NOW I'M TURNING MY BACK AND RUNNING AWAY AT FULL SPEED!
EVEN IF THEY BOTH TOLD ME THEY HATED ME...
WOULD I STILL BE ABLE TO TELL THEM I LOVE THEM?
WOULD I BE ABLE TO CHOOSE WHICH GIRL I LOVE MORE?!

NOTHING'S CHANGED, AFTER ALL.
I CAN'T TRY WHEN IT REALLY MATTERS UNLESS I ACTUALLY LOVE THEM.
WHEEZ
ALL I'LL EVER BE CAPABLE OF IS PROTECTING MY VULNERABLE SELF.
WHEEZ
WHEEZ

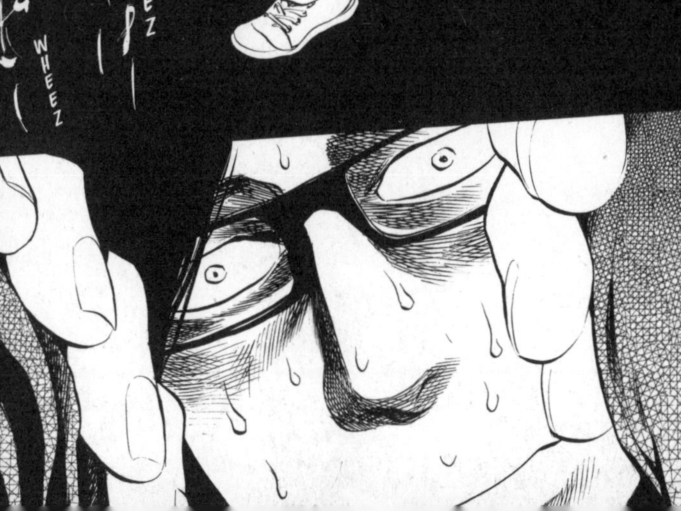

Shit ...
Why am I remem- bering her now ...?
WILL I EVER BE ABLE TO LOVE SOMEONE MORE THAN THE WOMAN I LOVED MOST OF ALL?

Just let me forget about heeerrr !!
THE SUN WENT DOWN AS I WAS LOST, AND THE PATH AHEAD HAD NO LIGHT !
NOW I'M SEARCHING FOR SOMEONE'S FOOTSTEPS IN THE BLACK OF NIGHT!
Whoa, you're really into this song ...
Itsuka, you can sing Izumi Tachibana songs?!

chapter 18 ♥ END

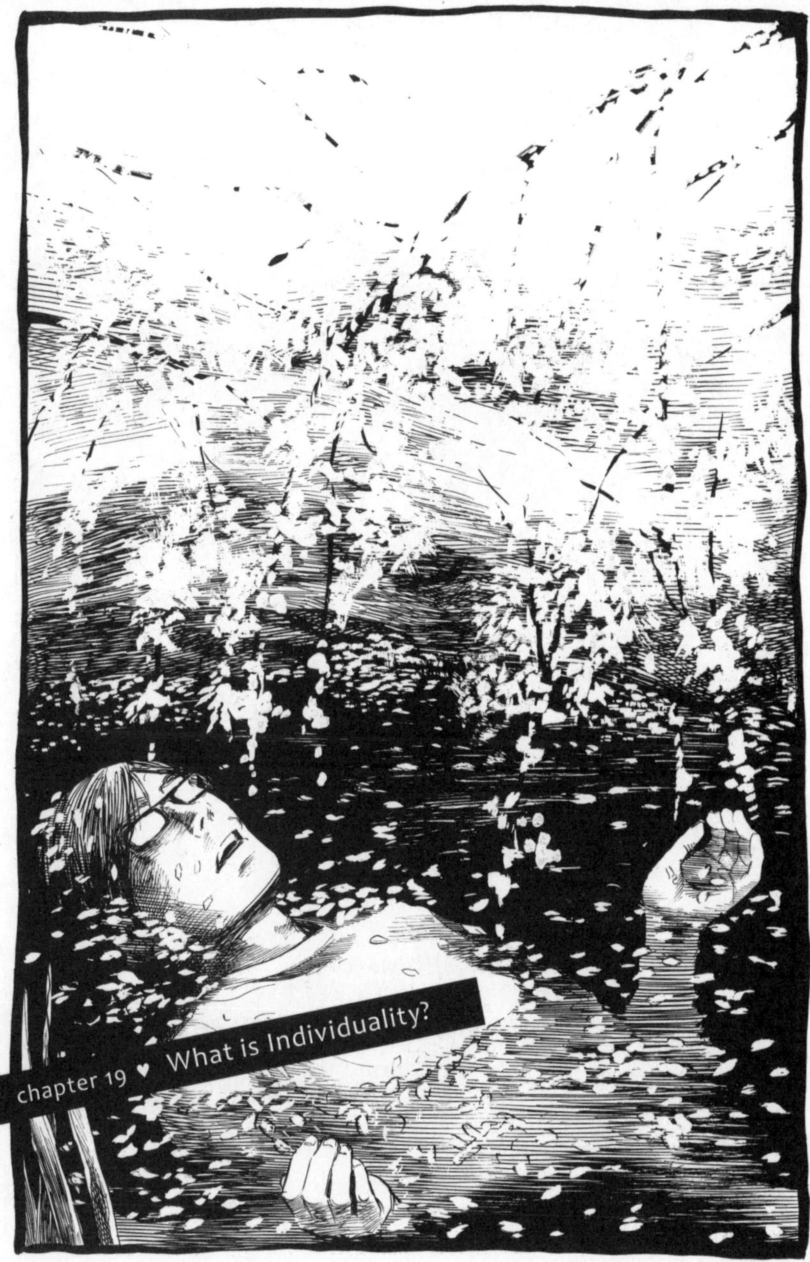

chapter 19 ♥ What is Individuality?

Hey, take my picture with your phone! ♡
Hey, Naaa-ooo!
This is NTT. The number you have dialed is...
...if you would like to leave a message ...

Fuji-moto!

I haven't heard from you in a bit. I'm worried about you.

You dead? If you're busy 'cause you got a girlfriend, tell me.

You can even text me. I just wanna hear back from you.

BIP

C'mon, Nao!

Whoa!

You look kinda sad...

Did that guy not pick up the phone again?

How dare he just go silent ever since winter!!

Why the hell is he making me worry?!

What if he's dead?!?

I wonder why...

...

Nao, can you give me your phone for a sec?

FUJIMOTO
Sub HELP ME
This is Yuma
Nao just got hit by car and won't stop bleeding, what should I do?!
Nao's gonna die!!
KLIK
KLIK
KLIK
Okay!
And... sent.
?

HUUSSSH
しーん

RING A LING
A DING
VVT

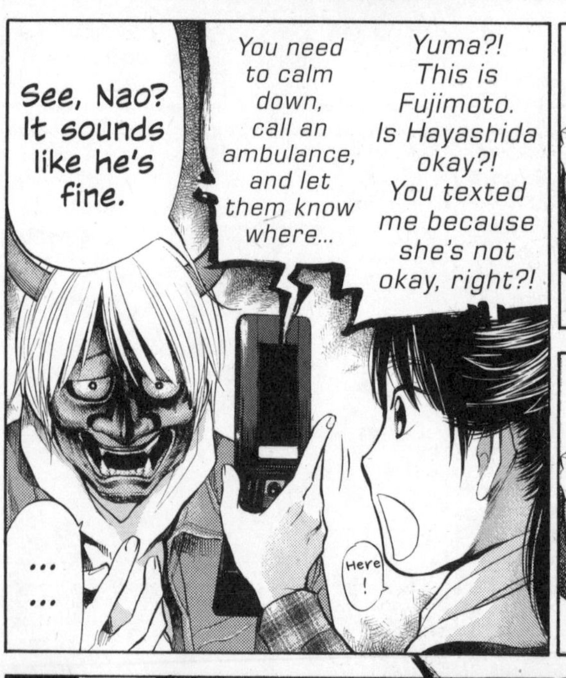

Yuma?! This is Fujimoto. Is Hayashida okay?! You texted me because she's not okay, right?!
You need to calm down, call an ambulance, and let them know where...
See, Nao? It sounds like he's fine.
Here!
... ...

FUJIMOTOOOOO
Whoa!

How long are you gonna run away from me? Is it something I did?!
If you can't get in touch for some reason, you could at least tell me without saying why.
Sure, I went too far when I said to beg girls to let you screw them, but...
... ...
it's not like I'm gonna kill you 'cause you aren't sleeping with anyone...
Hey, are you listening to me ?!

It's fine. You can just ignore me from now on.
I'm grateful to you, Haya-shida.
Sorry for making you worry all this time.
I'm okay now.

Huh?
Listen, what I'm tryna say is...
You're okay? How, exactly?!
See you.
G-CHAK
What did he say?

Y' know ...
I guess he'll be fine on his own.
I've meddled in his life enough.
パタン
PTAK
Is there anywhere you wanna go during break, Yuma?
I wanna see an alpaca!! I saw one on TV, it was all fluffy and super cute! ♡
Alpacas? Not capy-baras ?
I wonder if they're at the Bio Park!

So I've already tracked down his home. He lives around here.

DING DONG
DING DONG
DING DONG
DING DONG

I know you're there, Fuji-moto! Get out here now!!
We came all the way here to Tokyo! I took paid leave for this trip!!
It costs more to come here from the western edge of Japan than it does to go to Korea!
We got here last night!
BAM
BAM
BAM
We're going on an alpaca tour!! We already booked a bus, so hurry up and get ready, dammit!!
Alpacas are super cute!
BAM

GA CHIK
Wait...
For real...?
Oh!

C'MON, HURRY, FUJI-MOTO!
Huh?!
Wait, what?!

VWOOOM
It's spring! You gotta get out, feel the vitality of the land, and turn your spirits around!!

There's still snow on the mountains!
Ah, I'm just glad you're doing okay...

アルパカ牧場
ALPACA
XING
ALPACA FARM
Look, Nao, look! There're so many alpacas !!
They're soooo cute!
They really are super cute!!

Alpacas are herbivores, so they don't have a violent temperament or any weapons! They're timid, cowardly animals, and the only thing they can do is hurl their stinky spit at you when they feel scared!!
Huh!
So they're like me!
...
...
C'mon, Hayashida! You can say it, I don't care!!
SKREE
Wah!
SKRWRR
TWITCH
JOLT
TWITCH
JOLT
Wh...
What is that...?
SKRR
SKRR
SKRR
That's a warning sound.
TROMP
TROMP
TROMP
TROMP
SKREEEE

STAAAAARE
Stop it!
Don't look at me like that!
Even you guys are going to rep-rimand me?!
Fine, just spit on me!!
Y'know, this is actually calming. He hasn't changed at all.
Truth is you ac-tually enjoy being this negative, right?
It's a form of genius to be this self-flagellating here, surround-ed by nature.
I'm not gonna lecture you at all. Not about getting fat or anything else.
I'm not your mom, you know.
I was just curious about what happened to you, so I came to see for myself.
I'm not forcing you to tell me.
If you want to hear something from me, just say so.
Today, though, let's just have fun thinking about how cute these alpacas are.
... Yeah.
SHA
SHAA

You can walk the alpacas, too.
THROB
Aahh! So cuuu-uute!
Aren't you a cute little thing!
So fluffy and warm!
もふもふ FLOOF FLOOF
もふもふ FLOOF FLOOF
It accepts me!!
I'm so glad I'm alive!!
No fair, uncle! Lemme play with it, too!
You can walk this one over here, Yuma.
come on, it's like animal therapy.

MY LIFE RECENTLY HAS JUST BEEN WORKING, EATING, AND SLEEPING.
I FELT THAT A GUY LIKE ME SHOULDN'T BE ENJOYING HIS LIFE.
I HAVEN'T CONTACTED EITHER OF THOSE GIRLS THIS WHOLE TIME, AND THEY HAVEN'T GOTTEN IN TOUCH, EITHER.
I GOT A NEW JOB, THINKING THAT I COULD AT LEAST TRY HARDER AT WORK,
BUT NOW I'M TOO BUSY TO HAVE ANY FREE TIME.
IT'S NOT LIKE I LOST WEIGHT BECAUSE OF THAT, THOUGH. THE STRESS FROM THE NEW JOB PLUS EVERYTHING ELSE MAKES ME BINGE-EAT BEFORE BED...
AGH, I'M TIRED!
GAH
GAH
GAH
SOOO TIRED!
POTATO CHIPS
BEER
NOW LOOK HOW FAT I GOT. I WEIGH THE MOST I'VE EVER WEIGHED IN MY LIFE! HA HA HA HA!
ONCE I LOSE SOME WEIGHT... ONCE I FEEL CONFIDENT IN MYSELF...
THAT'S WHEN I'LL CONTACT THEM. THAT'S WHAT I'D TOLD MYSELF.

AND BEFORE I KNEW IT, IT WAS SPRING.

Aahhh! They're so cute and white and fluffy!!
Look over here!
SPRING WILL STILL COME WHETHER OR NOT I GET FAT OR DO NOTHING.

COME HERE, I HAVE SOME FOOD FOR YOU!

You can tell they're used to this because they're so popular!

HEH
AND NOW I'M THINKING OF HER AT A TIME LIKE THIS? IT'S LIKE I'M CURSED TO REMEMBER HER FOREVER.

IF I'M STUCK WITH THESE MEMORIES ALWAYS BLOCKING MY WAY,

CAN YOU BLAME ME FOR NOT BEING ABLE TO CHANGE?

That's huge !!

Won't that get in the way?

Yeah, but that's just how it is.

For now.

ONCE I GET BACK TO TOKYO,
WHAT IS IT I WANT TO DO MOST?

HUH ?!

You're stay-ing over ?!

Yeah.

We didn't get a hotel.

Hey, Nao! I wanna go to Dibney Sea tomorrow !!

Oh, and the Ghibli Museum, and—

MAP OF TOKY

Oh, right.

Are you trying to avoid getting dragged into some kinda bloodbath if some chick suddenly drops by?

No ...

No one's gonna come ...

I haven't reached out to them in a while, and vice versa ...

Again ?!

JOLT

This is why you're so damn ...

... ...

Nope... I decided I wasn't gonna lecture you anymore...

... Huh?

Hold on, it's fine if you get mad at me...

Actually, I kinda wanted to get your advice...

A lot happened...

Hmm...

Whatever it is you want to talk about...

am I really the one you should be saying it to?

The worst outcome is you feeling satisfied just 'cause you talked to me...

Who's the first person you should be talking to?
Aren't there angry people who you haven't bothered to contact this whole time?
Think about it.

JUMP
...
Agh, I can't help it! I just start lect-uring you!!
I hurt both Itsuka and Aki Doi by running away from them in such an awful way.
When I really think about it, I should have accepted all of that.

Aki Doi
had always loved me and waited for me.
How awful of a man does it make me if I'm just now realizing that?

...

SHMP

It's okay.

Don't worry, there's no way she could've loved a man as selfish as you all that deeply. ♡

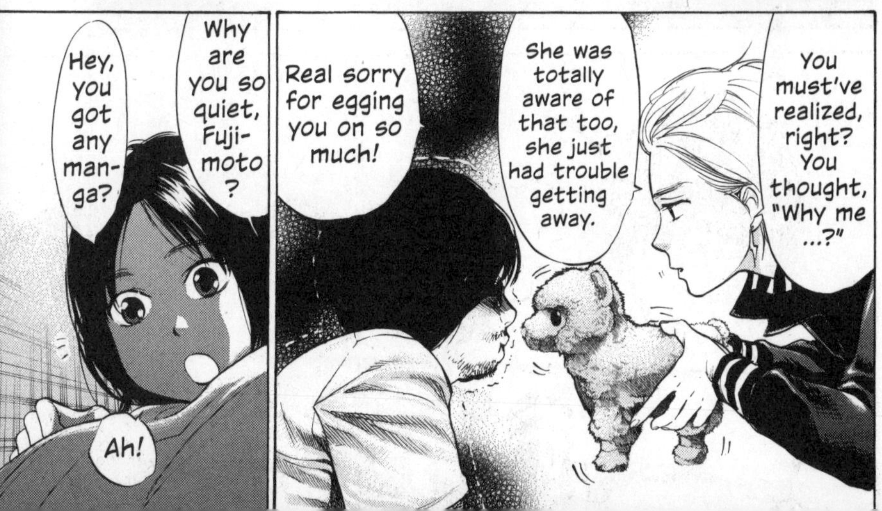

You must've realized, right? You thought, "Why me ...?"
She was totally aware of that too, she just had trouble getting away.
Real sorry for egging you on so much!
Why are you so quiet, Fuji-moto?
Hey, you got any man-ga?
Ah!

THE HEAD HOSTESS IS 18?!
5

WEEKLY SHONEN MAGAZINE EDITORIAL DEPARTMENT
THIS WAY
Editor-in-chief! Th-This is terrible!

It seems that Onosaka-sensei is heading this way right now...
Onosaka-sensei? How rare...
He barely shows his face around here, so why now...
SHONEN MAGAZ

He says he started a company recently, and he was coming to say hi...
A company?
How did someone who barely gets his manuscripts in each week find the time to start a company?
But, well, I'm mystified by how he's been meeting his deadlines...
About that...
Rumor has it that he's got a manager now...
Excuse us.

Wha
...?!
Is
that
you
...
Omu-
sensei
?!
NOD
Editor,
allow
me to
introduce
you to
my
manager.

Nice to meet you.

My name is Aki Doi, the manager at OM Inc.

Just watch me, Haya-shida!

I'm going to settle this all by myself!

I don't need your advice this time!

REA AAA LLY?

chapter 19 ♥ END

chapter 20 ♥ Rollin' Rollin'

Hey ...
Omu-sensei is actually talking and smiling!! The same guy who used to clam up for the whole 30 minutes at meetings ...
Who is that beautiful woman? Huh? His manager?
Is she the model for that new character?!
Those two have gotta be screwing. There's no way Omu-sensei could change so much otherwise.
Who *is* that woman?
The EIC doesn't know what to say!
Sounds like *The Head Hostess is 18?!* went to reprint again. Hasn't he gotten offers for a live-action adaptation?
They say he's had a few people ask.
It's popular, and it'll sell even more if it gets a TV show.
It'd be amazing if it happens thanks to that trophy woman by his side.

Omu-sen-sei.
Some-thing wrong?

Thanks for today.
I couldn't have come alone.

My manuscripts used to be late, I didn't get along with my editors, I couldn't talk to other authors...
It used to be that all I could do was draw manga all day. It feels odd, looking back now.

BEFORE THEY PICKED THIS SERIES UP, I USED TO COME HERE PRACTICALLY EVERY DAY, SPENDING ALL YEAR CORRECTING STORYBOARDS. IT GOT HARDER AND HARDER FOR ME TO UNDERSTAND WHAT I WANTED TO DRAW, WHAT I FOUND INTERESTING.

AFTER A MEETING WITH EDITORIAL ONE DAY
I HAPPENED TO LOOK UP.

SOME GUY WHO'D MADE HIS DEBUT THROUGH THE SAME CONTEST AS ME HAD GONE STRAIGHT TO SERIALIZATION, AND THEY'D GREENLIT AN ANIME, TOO.

THAT'S WHEN I GAVE UP.
I STARTED TO THINK THAT DRAWING BORING MANGA WAS A JOB, TOO.
SO I DECIDED TO FIGURE OUT JUST HOW BORING OF A MANGA I COULD DRAW.
屋形船へ行こう!

I STARTED DRAWING STORYBOARDS AND DIDN'T STOP, LIKE I WAS LASHING OUT AT SOMETHING.
I KEPT CREATING THIS ABSURD STORY, FULLY READY FOR READERS TO THINK IT WAS THE CRAPPIEST, DULLEST THING THEY'D EVER READ.

It got snapped up and was serialized in no time, but reader surveys showed mixed reviews. There were talks of cancellation.

I just kept drawing the manga like my life depended on it, though. I kept going, still unsure of what was actually interesting.

That was a year ago.

But now that you're here, manga has gone from something I nearly hated to something that's fun.

You reminded me of what it means to depict people.

I can't thank you enough.

I want
to try drawing inter-esting manga again.
And I need you to do that.
So if you would ...
Thank you very much ... I'd also like to—

KODANSHA
Oh, but ...
you're free to quit whenever if you get sick of it.

Sure, it'd be tough on me if you vanished, but I don't want to force you to stay in a bad situation.
It'll be a tough job, so I'm not gonna keep you against your will.
... ...
Ah ... I'm hungry!
How about Italian at the Four Seasons Hotel?
My treat, of course ...

OM (IN
TOKYO GAS

Good morning.
Good morning.
Good morning.
CHAK
Good morning.
Good morning.
Morning, Miss Doi!

Good morning.
The CPA is coming at 3:00, okay?

I knew that

A

ma

wo

You want him more than you want me, don't you? Do you hate me?

SKRITCH

SKRITCH

SKRITCH

SKRITCH

SNAP

Okay, Sensei! We'll be going now!
Thanks for today!
Omu-sensei?
Omu-sensei seemed stuck again this week.
Ugh, this might mean another all-nighter at the end.
Yeah.
It's gotten a lot easier at the studio ever since Miss Doi came, but ...
he's gotten really slow with his storyboards.
His manuscripts are fast, but they're pretty sparse...
Again ...?
ドキドキドキ
BADUM
BADUM
We'll lock the door behind us... Bye!

I heard reader opinion has gone down a bit recently.

wait...

Were those color pages to try to help that?

I dunno ...

SKFF

SKFF

SKFF

SKFF

Everything he's having that new character Akky do seems to be going over well, but it's like the lead, Yuzu, might as well not even exist.

Someone told me a *shonen* manga with an inactive main character won't be popular for long.

I overheard some of his editorial meeting ...

Ooh ...

ガタン
ゴトン
GTUNG
GTUNG

HSSSK
HSSK...
HSSK
HSSSK...
HSSK
野
のが
Nogat
都立家政
Toritsu-Kasei

?
GATA
STA
DASH

RAAARRRRRGH

Remembered he needed reference photos of a residential area
BIP BIP
BIP BIP
BIP BIP

AH!

Residential Area

HSSK
HSSK
HSSK...
HSSK

Hey, you ...
Just what are you doing?
BADUM
Why are you taking photos of someone's house?

Er ... Ah ...
Aaah...
Why are you not talking?
Don't make me call the police!
... gh!

I'm wiped out. That was my first time there. It's so crowded!

I'm never going back!!

But you were thrilled to cuddle with Nyaffy, Fujimoto.

Nyaffy was so cute! ♡

DOYA?

STROLL

Man, I barely recognized you without the hat.
And meeting you in front of my building, of all places! I'm thrilled!!
Oh, here's some coffee...
How great, Fuji-moto.
Wow, you two look a lot alike!
Aren't these cute?
Uh...
Ah...
DOYA?

Were you in the area for reference materials or something?
Oh, or maybe for some other reason?
SMILE

Yes... For reference...
MUMBLE
MUMBLE
And... Mr. Sumi... told me your address...

I... never gave you an autograph...

What...? You came out here just for that?!
Th-Thank you so much!
Oh, and I bought the latest volume, of course!
BUH BUH BUH!
Here it is.
DOYA?

...

So, Miss Doi... is your manager now.

I found out from this.

☆AFTERWORD☆
SPECIAL♡THANKS
MY MANAGER AKKY DOI!

Is she doing well?

I proposed to her yester-day.

She said yes.

WE'LL BE HAPPY TOGETHER!

THANKS!

Thank you very much ...

Well ...
I still have some work left to do.
Oh, thanks for coming by.

IN FACT...

BIP BIP

BIP

BIP BIP

I STILL HAVEN'T

SAID ANYTHING TO YOU.

PWAAAAAN
GTUNG
GTUNG
GTUNG
GTUNG
VWOOOOOOSH
...
KRIK
BAM

スル
SLIIDE
PTAM

PKAK
...

ドキ
BADUM
Ack!

YUKIYO FUJIMOTO
FORWARD
MUTE

What...?
Why now...?

Ugh...!
Everything is turning into a total pain in the ass...!

VVT
VVT
VVT
VVT

Hello?
Fuji-moto...?
BAM

Ah... ha haah... M... Miss Doi... It's been a while... Sorry for the sudden call...
?
Wh... Where are you right now...?

At home...
Why?

Uhm... I had a souvenir I wanted to give you... Is now a good time...?
Huh?
Now...?

You gave me your address before...
This is still the right one, isn't it...?
HAA
HAA
By the vending machine...

BA
MM

HAA
HAA
HAA
?
HAA
HAA

Ugh.
You're being super creepy ...

... Yeah.
I know.
HAA HAA

HSSK...
HSSK...
HSSK...

Still no story-boards from Omu-sensei ...
I'm gonna take him to the printer next time and show him all the trucks waiting.
SHONE
EDITORIAL DEPARTMENT, MAGAZINE

chapter 20 ♥ END

chapter 21 ♥ Native Dancer

Why ...
would you suddenly come all the way here ?
You know that this is only going to annoy me at this point.
So could you please go home?
Uhm... Could we just talk for a bit ...?
DOYA?
No.
I don't want to talk to you anymore, Fujimoto. Bye.

BTAM
TOONE
TOONE
TOONE
Ah ha ha ...
I didn't think she'd be *that* creeped out ...
I'm feeling totally creeped out myself now ...
Eh heh heh ...

Agh! No, no, no, no!
He's so scary!
He's so gross!
Was Fuji-moto always this much of a stalker?!

Who is that ...?
He's been there for a while now... So scary.

KLOP
KLOP
KLOP

Miss Doi ...!!
DOYA?

Could we do this over there? People will see if we stay here.

S... Sure.
This seems like it's gonna get heated.
Yeah ...
I mean, that lady is totally uninter-ested in his love right now.
Uhm ...
Wanna go to a family restau-rant around here ?
I want to take care of this here.
So what is it? Make it quick.

I'VE BEEN REJECTED AND IGNORED PLENTY OF TIMES BEFORE...
Girls are so nice!
YUKIYO FUJIMOTO IN HIS EARLY 20'S
She's clearly uninterested in me, but she's still talking to me...
Really, Fuji? wow!

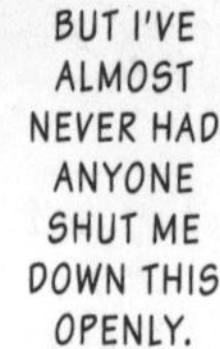

BUT I'VE ALMOST NEVER HAD ANYONE SHUT ME DOWN THIS OPENLY.

THIS IS THE FIRST TIME A WOMAN HAS HATED ME SO MUCH THAT
KRAKL
AN AURA OF REJECTION IS EMANATING FROM EVERY SINGLE ONE OF HER PORES!
ZZNAP...
I've never seen Doi look like that before... I'm sorry, I'm sorry, I'm sorry...

BUT EVEN IF THIS IS THE WORST I'LL EVER LOOK IN MY LIFE

DOYA?

I'M NOT LETTING THIS CHANCE GET AWAY FROM ME!!

I... I'm not a stalker or anything. I don't want you to get the wrong idea.
I'm sorry for surprising you.
But this isn't something I wanted to talk about on the phone. I wanted to meet in person because I want you to trust me.
You understand, right?

You lack common sense showing up this late, especially when you haven't contacted me in months.
PTAK
If you do anything weird I'm calling the cops.
AAGH!

DUN DUN DUN DUN DUN
I need to start by making her feel like I'm not her enemy!!
Ah...
Uh...
I want to settle this peacefully! I want to avoid a battle!!

Uhm!
Like I said on the phone...
RSTLE
I brought you a souvenir today!
RSTLE

Here!
A Nyaffy phone strap! ☆

Oh ...
Kids like those, don't they ...
Uh ...
Uhm ...
Erm ...
Wait, were you the type to go to Dibney Sea to begin with?

If you have another woman,
could you just leave me alone ...?
KRAKLE
Ah ...

You can't possibly think that I've just been obsessively waiting for you all this time we've been apart, right?
AAAAAH...
Since when have you been conscientious enough to go around trying to preserve your relationship with every girl who shows interest?

Sorry, I'm not the kind of cheap girl who'd be fooled by something like this.
Did you really think I'd be happy getting a souvenir you bought on a date?!

I don't need this.
I don't even like Nyaffy.
And there's no reason for you to give something like this to me anymore.
...
I...
I came here because I wanted to say congrats...
For what?
I heard you and Omu-sensei are getting married.
I happened to run into him today and he told me.

Huh?
I was shocked to see Omu-sensei looking so handsome...
That change was thanks to you, right?
Having a personal and professional partner seems so great. Yep, I think you two are perfect for each other. I'm so glad, so glad.
MUMBL
MUMBL
MUMBL
Meanwhile, look at how fat I got since we last met...
Of course you'd be super creeped out. I get it.
It'd leave a bad taste for both of us if we let things end the way they did last time.
It's not like I'm here because of some lingering attachment, so don't worry.
I thought I'd let you reject me nice and properly...

SMAKK
Huh ...?
KLATTER KLATTER KLATTER
What ?!
THROB
... Aargh ...
Geez ...

How desperate are you to turn me into the villain ?!
What should I say? "I hate poor, talentless, cowardly, self-absorbed fatsos with no dreams! Fuck off and die!!"? Would that make you happy?!
Did you come here so you could tell yourself that women really do just go for talented guys with money and pride?!
If you think I can turn around and happily get married after you do this to me, you're sorely mistaken!
Well, if you love being down on yourself that much, then why don't you go off and die of guilt?! Moron!

HAA

HAA

HAA

Ah.

I'm not crying right now. And I don't want your attention, either.
BAM
Uh.
Okay.

?
Voices ...?
A fight ?
Maybe I should call the cops ...
AH!

...Uhm. Well, I'll get going.
NOD
Uh... Yeah, could you ?

I needed to be really motivated to work up the courage to talk to you.

So thank you.

In the end,

I guess we never talked about anything.

Miss Doi,
let's talk about all sorts of things. As friends.

...

Sorry for the fuss.
Oh... No...

That wasn't enough!

What was with that "Look at me, I'm so cool, I accept reality" act? Ugh, I'm so pissed!!

And really, Omu-sensei?!

What's this nonsense about getting married? Is that what happened yesterday?!

SLAM

I barely got to chew him out at all!

I don't get it!

That wasn't a proposal! And why say that to Fujimoto?!

I gotta set the record straight on that at least!
BAM

He can't be far ...

Uh.

...
What are you doing ...?

Ah ...
Looking for the glasses you sent flying ...
The trains have ended, so I was scared of walking home without them.

...
...

Ah.
Here they are.
Really?! Thank you!

...
DOYA?

Miss Doi?
Would you want to... get something to eat?
I can pay if it's like 1,000 yen.
There aren't any family restaurants around here...
VULTURE PUB
BOOM

HUNH?!
And so this Hayashida person got you so worked up that you decided to talk to me again?
I was feeling lonely, too!
What's the problem? It's not like anyone loves me right now. You wouldn't be interested in a fatty like me either, right?!
So it wasn't just Itsuka?!
You're the worst!
BAM
BAM
Argh, how many times are you gonna do that self-deprecating routine?!

Uugh...
Now I have a complete picture of you and all your relationships with women, Fujimoto.
I can't believe I was the one that got you thinking you were having your *moteki*...
Oh, but thanks to you...
my life finally started to change. Women never used to be interested in me...
I guess I should say thanks for letting me dream.
HRMF
HRMF
Mind if I smoke?
Can I get a cig, chef?

Oh, not OK?
It's fine. I just didn't realize you smoked.

Only when I'm drinking or when I'm out. I rarely smoke now.
I smoked more when we worked at the same place. You didn't know?
Wait, really?

ODEN
SMELT
...
You really weren't paying any attention to me, were you?
Back then, I mean.

Ha ha ha ha...
It's not just you. I'm clueless when it comes to any nice, proper, pretty woman.
It wasn't malicious. Don't be mad.

It's not like I'm smoking because of problems with my relationships or with work, y'know.
Just to be clear!!
Oh, really?
I figured you were having a rough time with something right now...

Are—

Are you really getting married?

Yep. I so am.
I'm totally getting married.
We're having tons of sex, like, every day. We're surprisingly compatible, from the office to the bedroom.
Thanks so much for introducing us, Fujimoto.
WAAAAAGH!
I DON'T WANNA HEAR THAT!!

Just what is he picturing right now...?
I'll let him wallow in it for a bit longer...
Another one, please!

AND NOW WE CAN FINALLY BE REAL FRIENDS.
Let's have a few more at my place!
Let's buy something at a corner store.
Huh? You sure?!
I paid back there, so you'd better treat me next time!
And you'd better get me a wedding gift since we're friends!!

AKI DOI PROBABLY DOESN'T SEE ME AS A MAN AT THIS POINT.
I SHOULDN'T LET MYSELF FALL IN LOVE WITH HER NOW.
DOYA?
WE CAN FINALLY BE OPEN WITH EACH OTHER WITHOUT HAVING TO WORRY ABOUT ANY OF THE MANEUVERING THAT COMES WITH ROMANCE.

ROMANCE ISN'T JUST FRIENDSHIP TAKEN A STEP FURTHER.
WE'RE ABLE TO BE FRIENDS NOW BECAUSE WE CAN REST ASSURED THAT ANY ROMANTIC TIES HAVE BEEN CUT.

What's wrong?
Not coming in?

... Okay.
Pardon the intrusion ...
DOYA?

WE'RE FRIENDS.
IT'LL BE OKAY.
BTAM

What? It's your first time coming over to a woman's place?!
I would've lost my virginity a lot earlier if it wasn't!!

Really... when I was at work, I kept quiet and I tried not to make any waves. I even made tea for everyone!
I was so desperate back then to avoid making anyone hate me!! Personalities change, y'know!
AKI DOI IS LETTING ME INTO HER HOME BECAUSE WE'RE FRIENDS.
Huh ...
But doesn't it defeat the purpose if that made you unable to get to know any of the girls better?
...
WE'RE FRIENDS,
WHICH IS WHY SHE'S LETTING ME SEE HER LIKE THIS.
This singer looks like you, Fujimoto.
What? Really?
Y'know, when I'd watch music shows like this one last year,
I'd always pay more attention to the plain-looking guys with glasses and black hair.
I was aghast when I realized it was 'cause they looked like you.
Wha ?!
BFFT

It's not like you were my type at all...

I guess it started after Fuji Rock.

This sort of thing has happened before...

Where I'd find myself chasing after people who looked like a guy I used to know even though I wasn't interested in him, and we never dated.

AREN'T YOU GETTING MARRIED, AKI DOI?!

I started to notice people who looked like you.

I wonder what it is.

Could that mean I really loved him after all?

WHUMP

I'm 27 now...
IS SHE SAYING THIS NOW BECAUSE WE'RE FRIENDS?
I was thinking maybe now is when I can fool around with guys who can't think about marriage...
Yaawn... Fuji-moto, you... mmm...

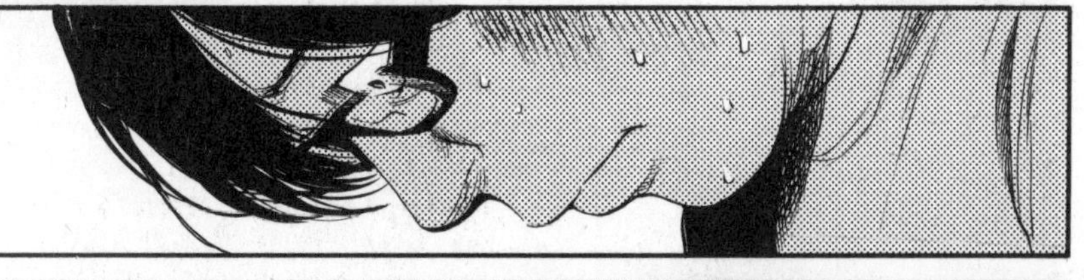

HOW SHOULD I FACE HER

AS A FRIEND?

I DON'T KNOW ANYMORE.

chapter 21 ♥ END

chapter 22 ♥ Cutting Edge

WHEN I FIRST MET AKI DOI,
SHE WORE NORMAL CLOTHES LIKE OTHER WOMEN WORE,
SHE HAD NORMAL RELATION-SHIPS WITH NORMAL GUYS WITH STEADY INCOMES,
HAA
AND SHE LOOKED LIKE SHE NEVER HAD TO DEAL WITH ANYTHING EMBARRASSING OR VULGAR.
...!
WELL, THAT'S HOW I SAW HER.
HAA

... Mn.
HUH?
HAA
HAA
Fuji-moto ... Wait.
WHAT AM I DOING RIGHT NOW?
I said wait.

Sorry.
I can't do this after all.
HAA
HAA
HAA
I can't handle this ...
right now ...

HADN'T AKI DOI REJECTED ME ALREADY?

......

I feel gross... I'm gonna puke.

AREN'T I DOING THE WORST POSSIBLE THING I COULD DO RIGHT NOW?

Get off of me ...

Don't get married, Aki Doi !!

WHOMP

?!

KREAK

Seriously ... I can't ...

Get off ...

I'm gonna puke ...

URP

... oi.
Miss Doo-ooi!
Are you okay?
Mmh ...
Yeah ...
Want some water?

I'm sorry for doing that when we're supposed to be just friends.
I'll talk to you later once I'm calmer.

バタンッ
BTAM

バタ
THUP
バタ
THUP
バタ
THUP
...

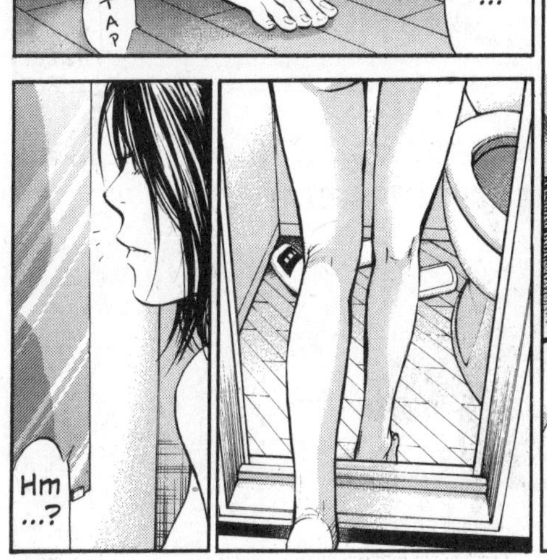
PTAP
Bath-room ...
Hm ...?

BOOF

Whoa!

Why do I look like this?!

Oh god...

My skin looks awful...

My face is swollen...

This is worse than if I didn't have any makeup on at all...

...

Uuuuuuuuuuuuuggh...

VWOOOOM
I wish I was listening to some-thing...
GATATANG
Other-wise,
I wanna fuckin' die ...
I FEEL LIKE THE STUFF IN MY HEAD
GATATANG
IS GONNA LEAK OUT...
GATATANG
GATATANG

Sorry, everyone!

I couldn't sleep with Aki Doi!!

JAPANESE REPRESENTATIVE

Whatta shock! I mean, can you believe it?!

I tried, but couldn't! At this point, that qualifies as a special skill!

This is the third time I've seen a girl naked but still couldn't do the deed with her!

Isn't that amazing Mr. Handsome Salaryman?!

But that's not what I want to talk about right now!

Yes, that was embarrassing!! It was totally cringe-worthy!!

That was my Super Deluxe level of ugliness, both inside and out!

I don't even need to wonder if she thought I was gross! I'm sure she did!!

No matter how many times I get rejected by a woman, it still hurts so much I wanna die!

But!!

SKRTCH SKRTCH

I ...

PSSHHH

THP

What do I tell Haya-shida ...?

I didn't text her what was happening, just that I'd be back late...

UNAGI

I'm home ...

BTAM

Huh?

They're not here?

I wanna go some-where fun...
ボスン
BSHOOM
Ah ...
So sleepy ...
...
I need to take a bath, change, then go to work ...
A bath ...
SHAAAA
アアアアア...
Are you okay?
I can't see anything, my glasses are fogged up!!
シャアア
SHAAAA
じゃぶじゃぶっ
SPLASH SPLASH
Bring me the duvet cover, I even got puke on that~!!
You, too, Fuji-moto! Take that off!
Huh?!
I'll wash it!
It's gross, right?!
I feel like I shouldn't do this with some-one who's about to get married, so, uhm...
IT'S A LITTLE LATE, BUT...
I'm not getting married!!
There's no wedding, there hasn't even been a proposal!

Huh...?!
THAT WAS A LIE?!

I didn't know either. We're not even dating!

He might see me that way 'cause I'm the only woman in his life...

but I was only with him on a professional level.

BADUM

I'm not interested in him like that, anyway.

I wanted to quit my last job after I was dragged into a bunch of personal drama and it got tough being there.

I became the manager at Omu-sensei's place because I wanted a job that felt fulfilling,

but his work pace is slower, possibly because of me ...

I want to help, but it's not like I can draw manuscripts.

Omu-sensei is trying to only give me the easy tasks.

Both you and Omu-sensei don't want to get deeply involved with me at all.

Don't... be so scared of me.

Argh ...
Crap ...
What should I do?
Aki Doiiii ~~
I shoulda done it with you ...
I wanna call you ...
I wanna see Aki Doi ...
I wanna see her so bad ...

SENT MESSAGE
OMU ONOSAKA-SENSEI
This is Doi
Hello, Sensei. I'm very sorry but I'm not feeling well, so I won't be coming in until the evening.
Okay ... Sent.

GWOOM
GWOOM
Ah... I guess I'll go in the evening ...

Don't get married!

AAARGH~!
Why is this happening again, after all this time ?!
Couldn't you at least come back when you're skinny?
THWAP
THWAP
BOMF
BOMF
I've never done it with a fat guy before!

You know ...
I really need to calm down ...
Fuji-moto isn't the only guy I know ...
Yeah !!
VVT
VVT
VVT
VVT
VVT

PLOK
Oh... He replied.
Huh?
RECEIVED MESS
OMU ONOSAKA-SENSEI
<No Subject>
Roger.
It's a nice ☼ day out today, you should air out your futon ☺ You must've sweat a lot, right?
What the heck ...?
What's your deal, Omu-sensei ?

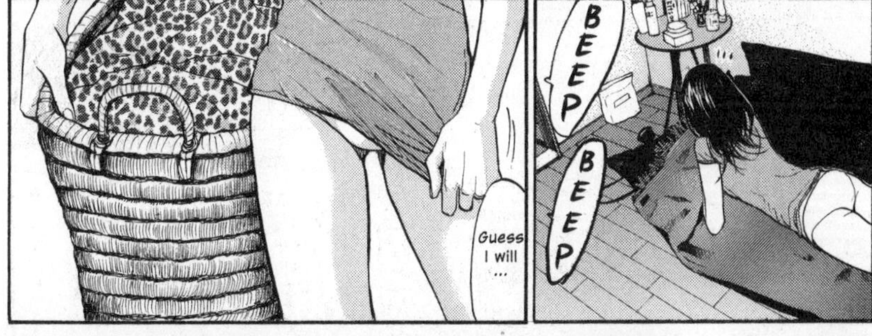
BEEP
BEEP
BEEP
BEEP
Guess I will ...

GACHAK
ガチャ
DO!

Here we go ...

SLAM
Huh?
What?
Was that...
really him? No, can't be...
ピンポーン
DING
DONG
JOLT

URGH
URGH
VVT VVT VVT VVT
INCOMING CALL
AKI DOI
WHOA!
Hello?
Aki Doi?!
VVT VVT -VVT
Aki Doi!
Miss Doi?
I was just thinking of calling you...
"I THINK IT WAS PROBABLY OMU-SENSEI.
GATATANG
THERE WAS NO ONE OUTSIDE AFTER THE DOORBELL RANG, EITHER..."
DASH

"BUT NYAFFY WAS HANGING ON THE DOOR HANDLE."
He probably saw what happened yesterday, too.
What should I do? He might come back. I'm scared.
Ah ...
I just invited Fujimoto over, but...
What ... am I going to do ?
AKI DOI!!
HEE
I'M COMING TO SAVE YOU!!
HAA
HAA
AKI DOI!
AKI DOI!
AKI DOI IIIIIIIIIII!!

BANG
ドッ
Miss Doi!
It's me!
BANG
ドドッ
BANG
Are you okay?
Fuji-moto!
HU
ガ
GG
ぎゅっ
I'm okay...
It's not like anything happened.
Oh, no... The way this is going... crap...

If Omu-sensei shows up,
I'll stay with you today.
I'll tell him I love you.

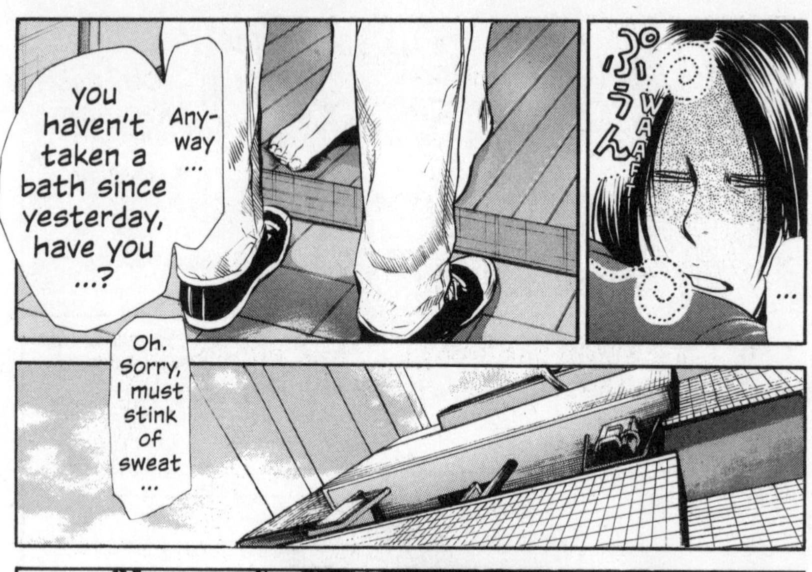
Any-way ...
you haven't taken a bath since yesterday, have you ...?
ぷうん
WAAFT
...
Oh. Sorry, I must stink of sweat ...
TRILLLL
Your call is being for-warded.
Please stay on the line.

Uncle?
This is Yuma, where've you been since yes-terday?
MUNICIPAL CENTRAL HOSPITAL
We're leaving today, okay?
TAXI STAND
We're visiting some rela-tives now.
I wish we coulda played more ...
Let's do some-thing fun again, Uncle!

Oh, and Nao says, "Don't overdo it."

TRILLL
TRILLL
TRILLL
TRILLL

Hey, Aki! This is Sumida.
Where are you right now?
Omu-sensei's editor came crying to me, saying he couldn't get ahold of him.
Has he gone off his manager's radar, too?

This is the first time he hasn't finished his storyboards with only two days until the deadline...
Could you at least tell him to pick up his phone?

THAT DAY,
FLASH
FLASH

OMU-SENSEI NEVER SHOWED UP.

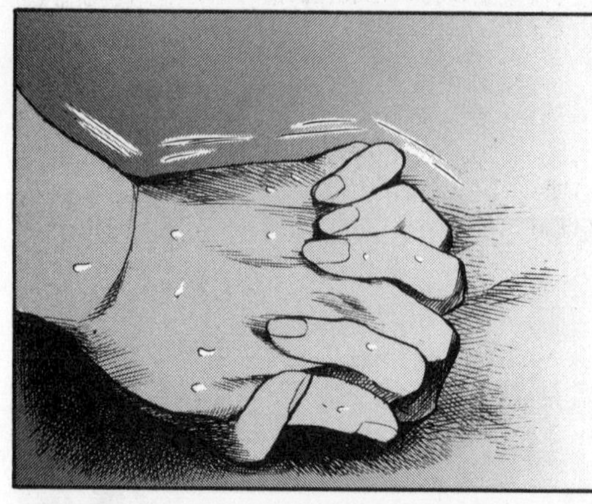
AND ALSO, THAT DAY, SHE TAUGHT ME A FEW THINGS I'D ALWAYS BEEN TOO EMBARRASSED TO ASK ABOUT.

Sorry.
Let me try one more time...!
This time, I'll...
Ah ...
You don't have to be in such a rush... I've heard it takes months before you can do it well...
Make me rush!
Please make me rush!!

AT 30 YEARS OLD,
I'D FINALLY REALIZED
THAT IT TAKES TIME
TO REALLY DIG DEEPLY
INTO SOMEONE.

chapter 22 ♥ END

chapter 23 ♥ The Rock 'n Roll Won't Stop Ringing

DAN
SH
Omu-sensei is still missing ?!
If his manuscript isn't in by morning the day after tomorrow, he won't be in the magazine!
BAM

MAGAZINE
He hasn't even done the storyboard, has he?
No.
It sounds like he was still at work yesterday, but when his staff came today, he was gone.
No one has been able to get ahold of him... This has never happened before.
We can't reach his manager, either, so we've split up into search parties.

Well, you should get a replacement ready ...
About that ...
His page count has been dropping lately, so there's no replacement that would be the right length.
HAAH
Urgh!
Ow, ow, ow, ow! The base of my big toe!!
Just one missing title is enough to make it hurt !
Aagh! Is your gout flaring up, Editor ?!
Hurry up and find Omu-sensei !!

24:00~8:00
30MIN/¥100
24H
Was he over there?
Nope...
I searched a bunch of book-stores and stuff, but no sign of him.
He really might not be around here...

Anywhere else you can think of?

Did he say anything the last time you saw him?

It seemed like he was stuck on the story-board, but...

He was treating Miss Doi the same as always, too. I wondered if he'd be okay, but...

...

I just hope he didn't get involved in some weird accident...

Can't you contact me, at least...?

Please...

just don't go off the rails and do anything to hurt your-self...

Omu.

7TH FLOOR, THIS BUILDING
INTERNET MANGA CAFÉ

KLIK
KLIK KLIK KLIK
KLIK KLIK KLIK
KLIK
KLIK
KLIK KLIK KLIK
KLIK
KLIK KLIK KLIK KLIK

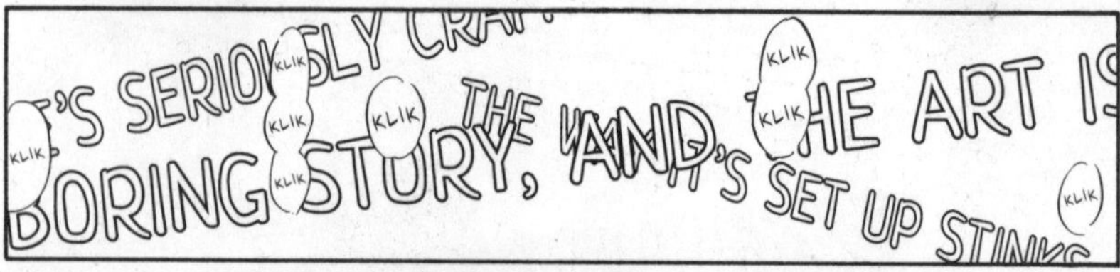
KLIK KLIK KLIK KLIK KLIK KLIK KLIK KLIK

Driven by a self-destructive impulse to read every single comment left on the internet about his work, something he'd always avoided.
Unh ...
Uunh.
HAA
HAA
Uuh!
Uunh ...!
Uuh ...

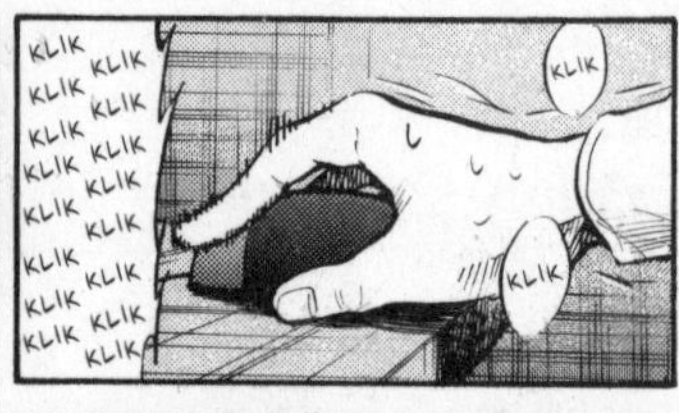
KLIK
KLIK
KLIK KLIK KLIK KLIK KLIK KLIK KLIK KLIK KLIK KLIK KLIK KLIK KLIK KLIK KLIK KLIK KLIK KLIK KLIK

SGRAASH
KABAMM
SMAAASH
Sir, is something the matter?!
Omu-sensei!
Why can't you do it? You kept saying you could!
Just how much trouble are you gonna cause us?!
If you've got the time for this, hurry up and get to work!
We've been holding back this whole time!
HSSHH
He soaked the place in gas and set it on fire!
RUUUUUN!
The manga is gonna burn...!
AAAAHH!!
Save meeee!
He wants to die!
He wants to die with his manga!
I SHOULD JUST DIE.
GROOOOAAAR
FSSHH
HSSHH

"I read this week's issue. I'm done with this series."

"I hope they kill this title soon."

"It's gotten so boring ever since the new arc started."

"Omu's gotta be a virgin, lol. He doesn't know a thing about real women, what a creep, ha ha"

...

Would rather insult himself than be insulted by others.

34 hours until the deadline...

...
...
...

SHAKE
SHAKE

RISE
むくり

ガリ
SKRTCH
ガリ
SKRTCH

Excuse me... Can I borrow some paper and a mechanical pencil ...

...
...
...
KLATTER
HMF!
Go over it once more...
Swap out this scene...
Shit, if only I had scissors and tape...
INTERNET
MANGACAFE

MUTTER...
MUTTER MUTTER
MUTTER MUTTER
MUTTER...
MUTTER...
OWL SPOT
Omu-sensei?

BAM

You're okay !!
I'm so glad ...
I just got in touch with Mr. Sumida ...
I'm sorry for being use-less as your manager when you needed me most...
I thought you'd be around here, Omu-sensei!!

...
ACK
What's wrong, Omu-sensei?!
Isn't your hair grayer than it used to be?
SHAKE
SHAKE
SHAKE

MUMBLE
MUMBLE
I just read an entire hate thread, including the archives...
Not looking at the internet is part of your job, Omu-sensei!!

Is that the storyboard...?
HURK

This... It's only... half-done...

Oh!

You've already finished half!

WHEW!

Don't you mean I've *only* finished half?!

If you keep saying careless things like that, they're gonna start shelling us from the Gokokuji building!

What do you want to do, then? Should we meet with your editor?
If you're going to draw the rest, how long should I tell him it'll take?
Uhm... with this content, then... well... I might be able to do it... in an hour...
Are you sure? Can you really do it in just an hour?
Wouldn't it be better if we said two or three?
But if it really only took an hour, that'd be great.
Urgh...
Then... two hours...
Got it.
I'll let them know!
Please go back to working on the story-board, Omu-sensei!
I'll try to help, too!
Your staff are at home on stand-by, so I'll call them when you're ready to give them work.
Huh?
No, go away!
Oh.
Hello? This is Doi.

Omu-sensei had a thought.

"Those two positively reek of the sex they were just having. Do they get a kick out of tormenting me like this? Die, die, die, die!!"

PRRING
PRRING
PRRING
BADUMM
...
Hello ...?
... Yes ?
Great work, Omu-sensei! I read every-thing!
It's great up to page 8, but we don't need the stuff past that.
Urk !
Are you trying to send some kinda message? I don't really get it.
Well ... It's, erm, uhm ...
Please re-do the second half of the story-board.
Is two and a half hours enough? Get the first half started, too.
This chapter wraps up the arc with the new character Akky, so we need the manuscript to look sharp until the last page!

Omu-sensei had a thought.

"Why isn't anyone getting mad at me or abandoning me?"

Whoa!! That's some wild hair...
Are you okay, Sen-sei?
Have you not slept?

"Why doesn't anyone ask me if what I'm trying to do is impos-sible?"

Here. Draw that.
Okay!
First take this from Kabuki-cho and...
SHRIP
Put this in here.

"I'm always the only one in the wrong, and everyone around me is always shockingly kind."

SKRIBBLE
SKRIBBLE
SKRIBBLE
SKRIBBLE
SKRIBBLE
SKRIBBLE
Is there anything you'd like to eat, Omu-sensei? I'll make whatever you want!!
Uhm, I...
I'M NOT HUNGRY!!

Omu-sensei still hadn't forgiven them, because the mere sight of this couple who'd probably just had sex made him feel like he was about to lose his mind.

But now wasn't the time for that.

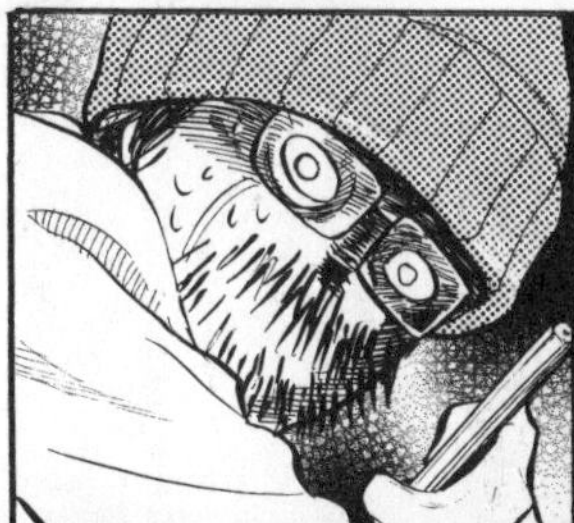

Miss Doi...
If I'm asking for too much, just tell me.
Hm? What is it?

Can you pose
like this?
outta my way!
I
the top hostess in this club!

YES!!
Like this ...?
...
KSHK
KSHK
KSHK
Look down on me more!! Yes, that's it!
Good!!
This is what I wanna draw!!
SKRIBBLE SKRIBBLE SKRIBBLE SKRIBBLE SKRIBBLE SKRIBBLE SKRIBBLE SKRIBBLE SKRIBBLE
SKRIBBLE SKRIBBLE SKRIBBLE SKRIBBLE SKRIBBLE SKRIBBLE SKRIBBLE SKRIBBLE SKRIBBLE
SKRIBBLE SKRIBBLE SKRIBBLE SKRIBBLE SKRIBBLE SKRIBBLE SKRIBBLE SKRIBBLE SKRIBBLE
SKRIBBLE SKRIBBLE SKRIBBLE SKRIBBLE SKRIBBLE SKRIBBLE SKRIBBLE SKRIBBLE SKRIBBLE

WHPP
Extract the lineart from this overhead shot of Kabukicho and make it look more hand-drawn!
Huh?! I've never done anything like that before!
Do you have CS or PS? I don't know how to use design software...
No!! Go buy it, there's a Bic Camera nearby.
All of you, start drawing the panels for the manuscript!
Okay!
Draw the Metropolitan Government Building and 100 hostesses for this two-page spread!
OKAY!
Make the background characters look like their nipples are harder!!
FSSHH
FSSHH
HAA
HAA
?!
What's wrong, Takashi?
Ah...
Are you okay?!

It seems he hasn't felt well since yester-day.
But he still looked for Omu-sensei with us...
NNNH
NNNH
UNNH

It's hard to find temp assistants with the chronic assistant shortage we've been going through. I'll keep looking, but I'm sorry in advance if I don't find anyone.

Hm?
Uhh...
HSS...
HSS...
Oops, that erased it!
CS GUIDE

AND I BROUGHT A HUNDRED HOSTESSES WITH ME!
...
...
...
...
Who has the refer-ence mat-erials for the club?
HUB
BUB
Ah, out of screen-tone! I'll go buy some!
Wait, they're closed at this hour!

BIP
BIP
BIP

TRILLLL
TRILLLL

Oh...
Hello...? Ms. Nomura?
It's been a while... This is Onosaka. Is now a good time?
You just finished work? Oh, I see...

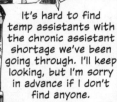

Wait... Ms. Nomura...? That assistant who quit after they got in a fight ...?
I think so ...
I know I'm in no position to ask you this, but...
Can you come over immediately to help out as an assistant ...?
Yes... Your current boss just finished his manuscript today... Yes...
Please.
I need your help.
DING
DONG
...
SULK
Hello ...
...
Been a while ...
Sorry. Thank you.
SHUDDER
SHUDDER

How much do you have left?
What? That many pages? That's impos-sible!
How are you on an even worse schedule than before?
Sorry ...
I need a hundred hostesses in Kabukicho in this two-page spread...
WHAT?!
Change the story-board and make it a dozen. You're out of time.

I can see why they fought, but... it's really nice to have her in this situation.
SKREECH
SKREECH
WORKS FAST
ZWAAAASH
WHEW...
Oh ...

You're actually trying to get along with people,
Omu-sen-sei.

SLIDE
Fuji-moto.
Finished with those back-grounds?
Yeah... some-how...
Sorry for taking so long... All I did was slow everyone down.
It looks like they have enough help now.
Ha ha. Good work.
A lot hap-pened since yester-day, huh?
Well... I might've gotten lucky, getting back on decent terms with Omu-sensei thanks to all of this chaos...
I wasn't sure how things would turn out when I thought he was a stalker, but...

I guess...
I feel kinda relieved now that I know he wants to prioritize his work and not me.

Yeah ...

It must be nice, knowing that there's a job that's perfectly suited for you.

I don't have anything like that.

Just as long as he doesn't get starry-eyed about chasing some kind of dream job...

First, lose weight!! Then get a steady job!!

Omu-sensei's editor negotiated with the printer to extend his deadline by six hours, and he was able to submit the manuscript just in time.

Great work, Omu-sensei!
Please get some rest!
THMP
THMP
THMP
Remember, we have another meeting at 10 p.m.!!
Great work, Sensei!
BATAM
Are you OK?

Sorry... I'm so sorry...
I won't do this next time....

Submit your chapter early next week, okay?

Good night, Omu-sensei.

Okay, I guess we'll clean up a bit and then call it a day.
You help out, too!
Tsk!

And these magazines?
Oh, put those by Sensei's desk, please!

NATSUKI KOMIYAMA...

chapter 23 ♥ END

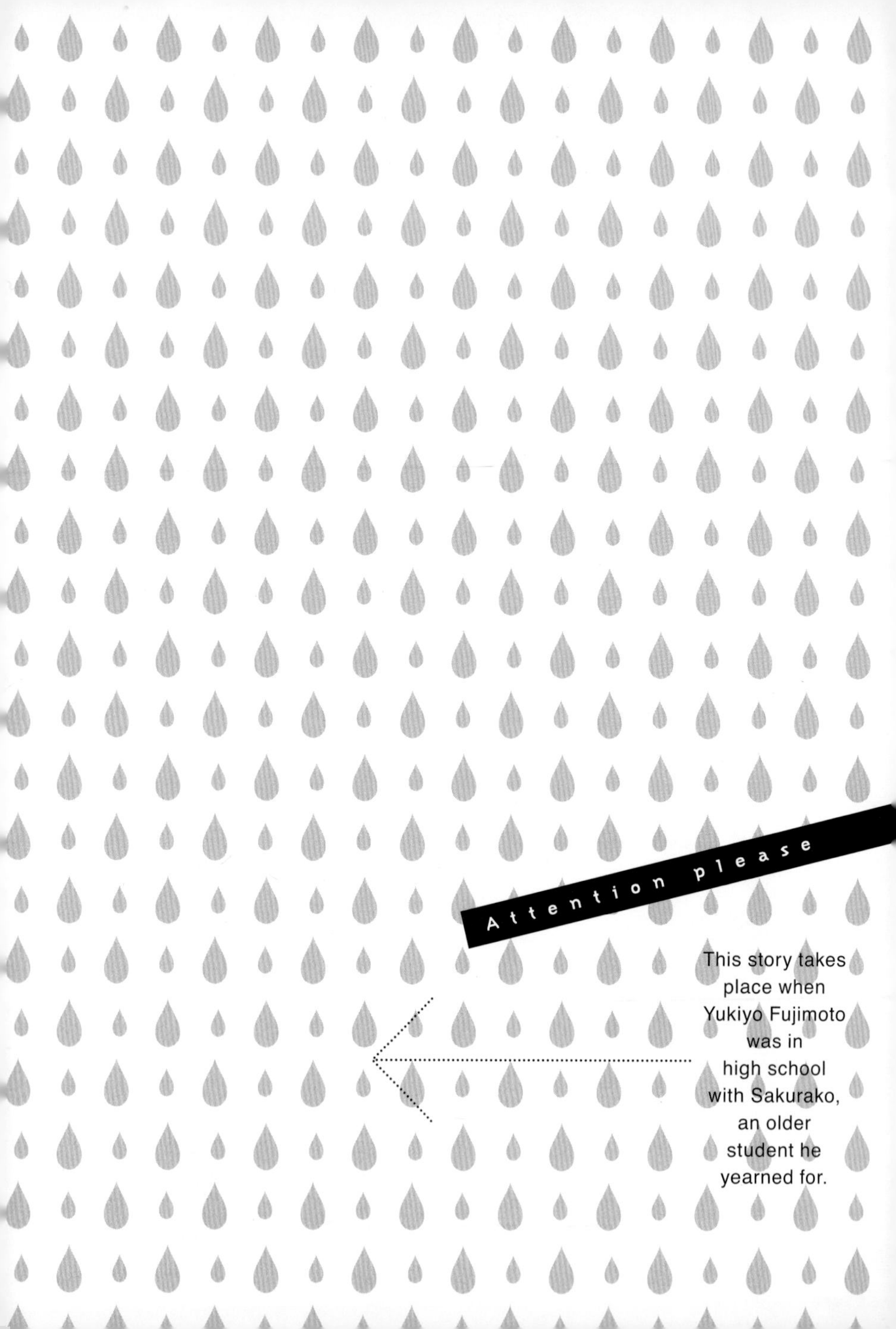
Attention please
This story takes place when Yukiyo Fujimoto was in high school with Sakurako, an older student he yearned for.

FOR SOME REASON, SHE WAS ALWAYS QUICK TO FIND ME.

WHENEVER I NOTICED SHE WAS NEARBY, SHE WAS ALREADY LOOKING IN MY DIRECTION,

AND SHE WAS ALWAYS

STIFLING A LAUGH.

Bonus Chapter ♥ Moteki: The School Days

What is it, Sakura-ko?
You might be a senior, but it's still rude to always laugh when you see me!
But you're just so funny!
You're always moving in such a weird way.
AH, THAT ONE REALLY GOT ME.
There's some-thing different about you, Fuji-moto.
You're so funny!
MY NAME IS YUKIYO FUJIMOTO. I'M A SOPHO-MORE IN HIGH SCHOOL
SAKURAKO IS TWO YEARS MY SENIOR.
...

Y' know, I think Sakurako might really like you, Fuji!
WHISPER
SNICKER
Shimada.
You think so, too?
WHISPER
You're not gonna tell her you like her? Seems like she'd totally say she likes you back.
BAM
BAM
...

SAKURAKO WAS THE STUDENT COUNCIL SECRETARY, AND I WAS IN THE RADIO CLUB. OUR CLUB ROOMS WERE RIGHT NEXT DOOR, SO I SAW HER A LOT.
STUDENT COUNCIL
It broke! Help me, Radio Club!
Again?!
RADIO CLUB
SHE'D COME BY THE NERD-FILLED RADIO CLUB A LOT, WHETHER IT WAS ASKING US TO FIX A BROKEN WORD PROCESSOR OR TO BORROW A TAPE PLAYER, AND WE SPOKE OFTEN.

Hey, I fixed it!

Sakurako?

Is she over there again...?

SHE LIKED TO GO TO THE EMPTY CLUB ROOM AT THE END OF THE HALL.

Sakurako?

SHE REALLY IS LIKE A CHILD.

Again...? I can't believe she can fall asleep on a filthy sofa like that.

What...? Again, teacher...?

Let's just study...

Mmh...

Talking in her sleep?!

Hey, what're you doing ?!
ビクゥッ
JOLT
Mrgh ...
Ah ...
ムクッ
RISE
Naka-mura from the soccer team ...
Oh, she woke up.

Did you have some-thing to ask the student council ?
Oh, right. Could we talk about that now ...?
SAKURAKO KNOWS PEOPLE FROM A LOT OF DIFFERENT CLUBS, SO SHE OFTEN GETS ASKED FOR ADVICE.
Sure we can.
THE TEACHERS PUT A LOT OF TRUST IN HER, TOO.

Ah!
Thanks for fixing my word proces-sor,
Fuji-moto.

AT FIRST,
I THOUGHT IT WAS JUST MY IMAGINATION.
PSHAP

SNICKER
SNICKER
Next door again ...

What is she trying to say to me ?
I'D NEVER EVEN TOLD A GIRL I LIKED HER BEFORE AT THAT POINT IN MY LIFE.
...

I WAS SO DESPERATE TO FIND OUT WHY SHE WAS ALWAYS LAUGHING AT ME.

Okay, I'll go get her! You just wait there!!

All right ... I'm counting on you, Shimada!!

I'll just casually ask her...

"How do you feel about me?"

"You don't like me or anything, do you?" WAAAGH!!!

AND THEN IF SHE SMILES THE WAY SHE ALWAYS SMILES,

I'LL TELL HER.

"In that case, will you go out with me?!"

I wonder how she's gonna look once she hears that~!

SLIIDE

Ah ...
BADUM
Uhm... I wanted to...
BADUM
BADUM
ask you something ...
BADUM
BADUM
I...
BADUM
FOR THE FIRST TIME,
I SAW A TROUBLED EXPRESSION ON HER FACE.

I DON'T REALLY REMEMBER WHAT HAPPENED AFTER THAT.

SHE QUIT THE STUDENT COUNCIL BEFORE SUMMER BREAK.
WE DIDN'T RUN INTO EACH OTHER IN THE CLUB BUILDING AFTER THAT.

I TOLD HER THAT I LIKED HER, AND I THINK SHE SAID SOMETHING ABOUT WANTING TO FOCUS ON ENTRANCE EXAMS.

Agh, I forgot my umbrella!

SHE DIDN'T LAUGH IN MY DIRECTION AGAIN, UP UNTIL THE DAY-BEFORE GRADUATION.

We can share.

So, today is graduation...

HAAZE

ROLL
ROLL
ROLL
I wanna die, I wanna die, I wanna die, I wanna die, I wanna die, I wanna die, I wanna die, I wanna die!

Acting like this since he asked her out
Ah... I think the words stopped meaning anything around the fourth time...
Eureka...
Heh heh...

I SHOULDN'T HAVE EVER TOLD HER HOW I FELT.
I WAS SO TOTALLY MISTAKEN. I'M SUCH AN IDIOT.
I'LL NEVER FORGET THAT BOTHERED LOOK ON HER FACE.
SHE WAS ALWAYS LAUGHING AT ME BECAUSE SHE WAS MAKING FUN OF ME.
URGH...

SLIIDE
DIE!
DIE!
SHIT!
DIE!
MY HEART...
DIE!
Ah.
You're here, Fujimoto.
Great timing. Can I ask you for a favor?
Huh?

?!

Ah! Hup, two, hup, two ...

What is this?!

A-Are you throwing-ing this out?

Yep.

Teach said a club is gonna be using that room soon so I should toss what we don't need.

This sofa's in tat-ters ...

So I thought I'd throw it right out along with
my memories of the damn thing!

Huh?
You have some kind of memo-ries tied to this couch?
What...? You never noticed, Fujimoto?
Noticed what?
Ugh, so heavy ...
... Oh ...
I was so sure ...
... that you had noticed ...

AH HA HA HA HA
Oh! Wow, I'm sorry for treating you so coldly!
Where did that come from?!
What?!
Fuji-moto...
You're gonna have a tough time when you're older. You really don't know how to pick women.
I hope you meet a girl who's really able to fall in love with you!!
?
Sure...
I DIDN'T REALLY UNDERSTAND WHAT SHE MEANT.
ドサ
WHUMP
ALL I COULD THINK ABOUT WAS HOW CUTE SAKURAKO WAS.
ゼーはー
WHEEZ
カチカチカチ
CHK CHK CHK
FWSH
Hm?

WAAAAAGH!
BWOOSH
Hot!
Hot!

SO PRETTY...
WOW!
...
ROOOOAR

What's that smoke?
HUB
BUB

WE KEPT THIS FIRE SCARE AS A SECRET BETWEEN US.

Oh shit!
Let's run!

I DIDN'T LEARN WHAT SHE MEANT UNTIL A LOT LATER IN LIFE.

Okay!

Ten years later...

Whaaat?! Sakurako was... in that room next door... For real?!

Everyone's spilling the beans in our school Mixi community right now!!

Makes a point of not checking Mixi

Aaagh! I never needed to know about that!!

Moteki: The School Days ♥ END

M o t e k i

M i t s u r o u   K u b o

Motekis You Wouldn't Want to Read ⑤

ZWOOOSH
ズウゥーン
BADUM
どくん
URGH!
Nobody who could commit rape would become a manga artist!
Right, Omu?
……
Ah, No way…

Motekis You Wouldn't Want to Read ⑥

EEEP!
I'm gonna die! They're gonna drop me!!

It's all done!
All right, gonna contact my editor...
BEEP
Oh, a fax ...

NOT FIT TO PRINT. -MAGAZINE
BOOOOM
......
This isn't even funny.

M o t e k i

M i t s u r o u   K u b o

MOTEKI

Love Strikes!

contents

Moteki
Mitsurou
Kubo

chapter 24 ♥ Get Up and Dance

Sweet Pieces for
These mains
this spri
from Beams. The blouse under it is
pale top paired with a brown jacket wil
is the key," says Natsuki Komiyama.
A street-style shot...? It really is her.
WHOA. WHOA ...!
JOLT
What's the matter, Fujimoto?
Er ... Uh ...
I was just wondering how much time Ebi-chan* had left in the limelight ...
You're the worst ...
Hurry up and clean

*model Yuri Ebihara

RIP
REALLY? WHY IS SHE SHOWING UP OUT OF NOWHERE RIGHT NOW?
JUST AS I WAS FORGETTING ABOUT HER...

Fuji-moto!

I want to get these boxes out of here while there's still a guy around.

Okay!

BUT IT'S NOT LIKE SHE MAKES ME FEEL ANYTHING ANYMORE... YEAH.

SHE DIDN'T EVEN MAKE ME BAT AN EYELASH!!

HMF

MOVING CENTER TRANSPORTATION

THE SON GOHAN OF MOVERS

HQ / TOKYO

0120-1XXXX

GRAK

?
Uuh ... ghh ...
Fuurrgh...

What's wrong, Fujimoto? Why are you mak-ing that face?
?!
Don't tell me ...!
Wh ...
Really ? The hospi-tal ?!
Can you guys help me?!
?
AAH!
AAH!

I NEVER THOUGHT IT WOULD HAPPEN.
...ACTUALLY, SAYING THAT WOULD BE A LIE. BUT I DIDN'T THINK IT WOULD EVER HAPPEN THIS SOON. I MEAN, AFTER ALL...!
WHAAAAAT?!
You're going back home because of a herniated disc?!
What about your job?! You quit?! Seriously?!
Yeah... I have to recuperate at home for a while...
I can't sit at a desk, so I can't do my job... and I don't have any savings... and I can't pay my rent... and I can't do any housework... I can't do anything,
so it's impossible for me to stay here in Tokyo like this.
THROB
THROB
THROB
I CAN'T BELIEVE
I REALLY HAVE TO LEAVE TOKYO.

Ichigaya
Wow ... Well, I guess you don't have a choice, then.
I know several guys who had to go back to the countryside because of herniated discs.
Take it easy, all right?

You're coming back to Tokyo once you're better, right?

SNIFFF
... Yeah ...
SHIMADA...
That's my plan ...

It sounds like there aren't any jobs out there in this recession. Just public servants and public works jobs.
Uh ...

I bet it's gonna be tough having to face people at home if you're unemployed... It wouldn't be as bad if you'd take any job you can get.
Uhm ...
It sounds like XX from high school took over the family business. He might have a job for you.
He runs a company now ...?
I forget, do you have a driver's license? It's impossible to get around without a car, y'know.
I'm begging you, I'm in an emotionally weak place right now. Don't make me any more anxious!

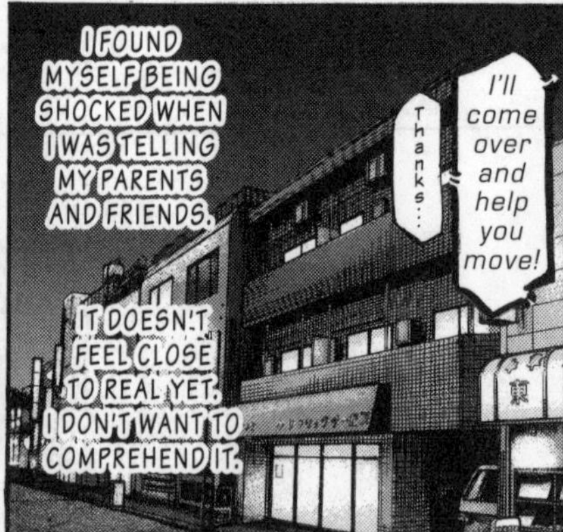
I'll come over and help you move!
Thanks...
I FOUND MYSELF BEING SHOCKED WHEN I WAS TELLING MY PARENTS AND FRIENDS.
IT DOESN'T FEEL CLOSE TO REAL YET. I DON'T WANT TO COMPREHEND IT.

BIP

ムカーッ
GRR

SHIT!
None of this would've happened if I hadn't seen you then...
SQUEEZ
SQUEEZ
SQUEEZ

...

RUSTLE
カサッ

Shit... How dare she look so truly happy...
I know she must be getting along with some other guy right now, anyway...
Hmf!

...

She... really does have a pretty face ...
Shit ...

DING
DONG
JOLT
... ?!

Were you asleep? Can I come in?

Is it OK for you to take time off from Omu-sensei?
Yeah, seems he's doing story-boards today.
I'll start packing your stuff up.

And ...
uhm, your moving day is the same day as Omu-sensei's deadline, so I can't be there to see you off...
Sor-ry!!

Oh! No, that's fine.
Shimada's coming to help, anyway!!
Don't worry, I wasn't really raised in a house that did send-offs.

What?
Are you in self-flagella-tion mode again?
I'm not.
I bet you are.
I'm not.

Nothing can start unless your body is all better, right?
This isn't the end, so you don't need to dwell on it so much!!

Take care of yourself, okay?
I ALREADY HAVE AKI DOI.
...I CAN SAY THAT, RIGHT?
Okay, is that every-thing?
Yep!
BTAM
VROOOOOM
Thank you for the help!
Heey! We're leaving, Fuji!
Okay!
HUP
BTAM

AT SHIMADA'S
All right ...
Here's to hoping you make a full recovery!
Th... Thank you ...

When is your flight tomorrow?
Uh, the afternoon.
Ah, I have work tomorrow. Sorry that I won't be there to see you off.
We'll visit home sooner or later, too.
Oh, and maybe I'll take a trip there!
I wanna eat a Sasebo Burger!
Me, too!
I've never left Honshu!

Oh!
By the way, Itsuka says to take care of yourself.
SIP
It sounds like she wanted to be here today but work got in the way.
...
SSIP
Seems like she's busy with work, but she's doing well.
It's like she wants to focus more on work than on guys right now!!
... ...
What shoot was she working on again? Oh! I love that director's work!!
Itsuka is so lucky!
It seems like I don't need to be around for people to enjoy their lives... That's good...
OOH!
AAH!
OOH!

KPOP
...

Oh, Fuji. That's right ...
Did you hear that Komiyama had a kid?

Wh... What?! She got married?!
I never knew that!
KOFF
KOFF
What? Really?
Seems it was a shotgun wedding. She sent me a postcard.

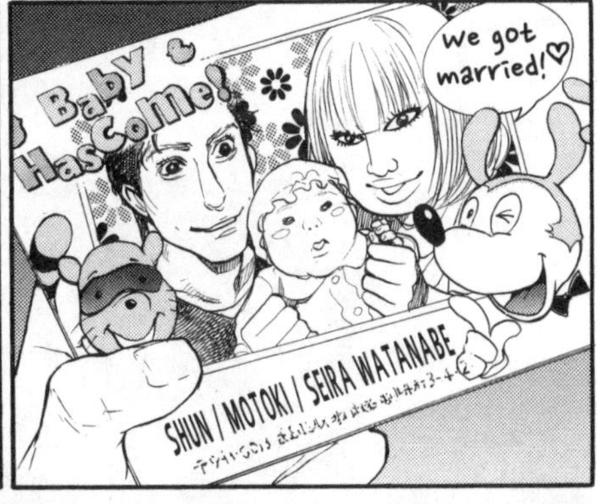
We got married!♡
Baby Has Come!
SHUN / MOTOKI / SEIRA WATANABE

Oh, he meant Motoki (the older one) ...
Still, I do feel conflicted...
If you're leaving Tokyo, why don't you at least reach out to her?

I FINALLY HAVE
AN EXCUSE TO CONTACT HER NOW.

YUKKII!
It's been so long! Why'd you change your number? You should've told me, dummy!
Ah ha ha ha, just kidding! I'm doing great!

It... It's nice to talk to you again...
What about you, Yukkii? Doing well?
Well, about that...
Wha? You're going back home? Seriously?! A slipped disc?
But I think it's good timing. Weren't you planning on going back eventually?
I got married back where I'm from, in Shizuoka.
SHAAAA
SQK

We're getting to the age where we need to start thinking about taking care of our parents.

If you can find a job back home, why don't you consider getting married over there?

Y... Yeah.

Uhm...

Speaking of... is Natsuki doing well?

She's still in Tokyo. You're not talking?
She said that she was worried about you.
... Oh ...
No, it's fine.
Yeah... Say hi to her for me.

Oh, let me put Shimada on for a bit.

Hey, Shimada! It's Motoki!

Ooh!

What's up! It's been a while!

IT'S NOT LIKE I'M INTERESTED IN HER ANYMORE.

AND AFTER EVERYTHING THAT'S HAPPENED, SHE PROBABLY DOESN'T EVEN... YEAH...

IN THAT CASE,

KLK

KLK

KLK

SEND

KLK

KLK

KLK

KLK

KLK

KLK

WHAT CAN I DO TO SETTLE THIS?

Message

NATSUKI KOMIYAMA

IT'S YUKIYO.

I'm going back to the countryside tomorrow. I won't be returning to Tokyo. I'll be waiting at Haneda until noon tomorrow.

MENU SELECT SEND

BUT TODAY
IS PROBABLY MY LAST CHANCE.

IF I CAN SETTLE THINGS HERE
I THINK I CAN GO BACK HOME AND START OVER FRESH.

SHE'S
NOT EVEN
REPLYING.

BAM

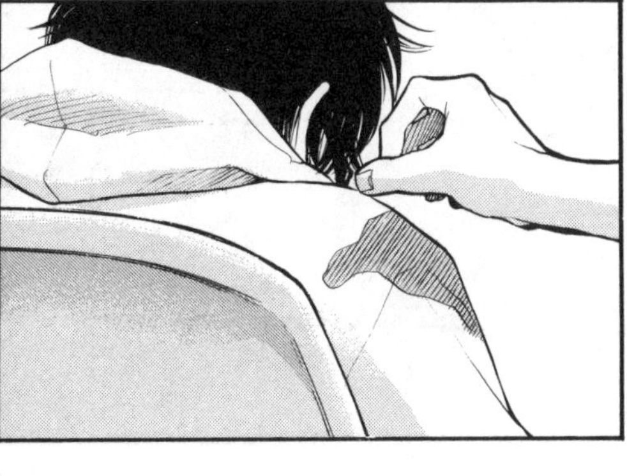

You dropped your cane.
Oh
Thanks ...
... Sorry.

THE GATE IS
IT IS NOW
WITH-OUT DELAY
BOONG
MOMMY!
AH HA HA
PLEASE MAKE YOUR WAY
QUICKLY
BOONG
BOONG
DEPARTING TRAVELERS SHOULD
TO FUKUOKA

...Boarding has begun for this flight. Please begin boarding immediately. Once again...

TRILLL...
TRILLL...
TRILLL...
BIP

TRI...

GACHAK
Hello ...? Yukiyo ?

Natsuki ...?

Yeah ...

Oh, sorry for not replying to your text.

I just woke up...

Oh, no! Not at all, I'm sorry for waking you!

She wasn't even trying to get here...

... ...

So... What is it ?

URGH

Ah!

I saw you in a magazine. You had a street shot published, right?

I was so surprised!

AH HA HA HA HA HA HA

Oh, so you saw that.

シーン… HUSSSH

...

...

IT'S NOT LIKE WE'RE EVER MEETING AGAIN, ANYWAY.

IT DOESN'T MATTER HOW MUCH SHE HATES ME!!

So! Do you have a boyfriend right now?

Whaat? Nope, I don't!

I do have someone I like, though.

ME ?!
Uh ... Huh ...
Wh- Who ...?
Some- one you don't know.
It's kind of like I've fallen in love for the first time in a while, y'know?

What about you, Yukiyo? Are you in love?

I'm not falling any deeper in love with you again!!
GRR
Ah ...
GRRRRR
Well ...
BUT WHAT IF I REALLY WAS STILL IN LOVE WITH YOU? WHAT THEN, YOU INSENSITIVE WOMAN?!

I'm ...

still dragging around my feelings for you ...

I hadn't told you all this time because I thought it'd bother you.

AGH!

You know how I feel about you, right? So why would you say that?

Oh, right. I'm your guy friend.

C'mon, stop it!

But I just can't do that. It hurts.

You're not going to hear from me again.

Don't worry, Natsuki. Bye.

... ...

Say some-thing !!

Come on !!

Take care of your-self.

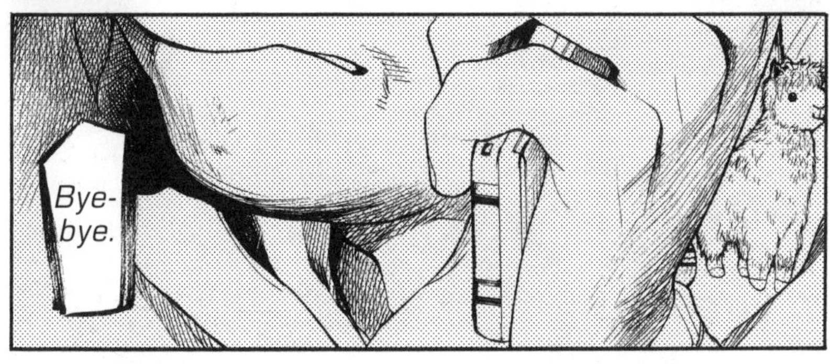
Bye-bye.

NATSUKI KOMIYAMA WAS THE WOMAN I LOVED MOST IN MY LIFE.
BUT IT'S NOT LIKE I HAVE A LOT OF EXPERIENCE BEING IN LOVE.

GROOOOAR
I'VE JUST HAD MY HEART BROKEN AGAIN AND AGAIN.
THAT'S ALL.
AND NOW THAT I REALIZE THAT,
I FEEL BET-TER.
YEAH.
GROOOAR
...
SLAM
SLAM
SLAM
I don't feel better at all !!
WHY DID I SAY THAT ?!
I CAN'T BELIEVE MYSELF!

GROOOAAAR
ゴォォォォ…
Yuki-yo!
Yukiyo? Are you not around?
MREEEN
MREEN
MREEN
CHITTER
MREEN
MREEN
MREEN
I'm sorry, it seems that he's out right now.
I'm sure he's not far, though.
Oh, okay.
Where did he go in this heat?
Is he better already?
He hasn't said hi to me at all since he got back.

chapter 24 ♥ END

chapter 25 ♥ Wounds Inside My Head

Stay inside ...
the white lines ...
or you die ...
Whew ...
Ha!
TOTTER
?!
WAAGH!
WHOOOO
WHOOSH

IT SEEMS A FEW MONTHS HAVE PASSED SINCE I CAME BACK TO THE COUNTRYSIDE FROM TOKYO. ARE YOU ALL DOING WELL?
WAAAAAHH!
I DON'T WANNA DIEEE!
...
...
JUMP
Okay!
Yep!!
Now that was a work-out!
Wanna call the cops?
Who is this guy?
I'M DOING GREAT ROTTING AWAY HERE IN RURAL JAPAN!!
Hey, that's the guy who showed up at old lady Fujimoto's house all fat!!
Huh? The guy that mom was calling a useless bum?
...

Kaya
Whew...
Hot...

This hamburger place
is as popular as ever!
Excuse me. My name's Hayashida, I called in an order.
One special burger and one chicken cutlet. Is it ready yet?
Yaay! ♡

Oh.
Nao, over there.
Huh?

ACK!
DID SHE NOTICE ME?!

SHOWA RAL
FUJI-MO-TOO-OOO?!?

Why are you runnin'?
SNAP
SNAP SNAP
My hair!
Stay off my back, too!
So, having fun staying holed up in your room and never coming to see me ever since you got back home?!
I see you're still not able to think of anyone who isn't yourself.
BAM
BAM

AFTER HERNIATING MY BACK IN THE SPRING,
I'D BEEN AVOIDING HAYASHIDA, WHO LIVES IN MY HOME TOWN.
ACTUALLY, IT WASN'T JUST HAYASHIDA.
I HADN'T SEEN MY OLD FRIENDS AT ALL EXCEPT WHEN THEY CAME TO CHECK UP ON ME, AND I WASN'T GOING OUT AND HAVING FUN WITH ANYONE, EITHER.

When'd you lose all that weight, Fujimoto?
I guess I lost a lot of it once I stopped being able to move around...
But my doctor said I shouldn't lie in bed all day and told me I should do some walking to put on muscle.
with a goal of 7,000 steps a day...
And I think I should start looking for a job...
Huh! What kind of work?
Ugh.
I'm not sure yet.
There aren't any jobs around here... Part of it must be the recession, but still...
The pay is way less compared to Tokyo, too...
So you're going back to Tokyo?
URGH...
DRIP DRIP

Speaking of Tokyo, what's going on with Aki Doi?
We've got a great long-distance relationship!! ♡
I gotta cherish my first girlfriend, right?

Oh, that's great!
She'll kick you to the curb if you're unemployed, though.
Even if you look better now, you gotta have a job!
Oh, did I hit a sore spot?
...
...
Well...
If Aki Doi dumps me,
can I have Yuma, Hayashida?
HA HA, JUST KIDDING!

I was joking, sheesh...
Please don't look at me like that.
It truly hurts...
Well, let's go drinking once your back feels better.
We should go back to Fumiko's place!
I'll introduce you to my drinking buddies...
Buruko

HAYA-SHIDA IS
AS CARING AS EVER.

She really looks out for me...
And I'm sorry, but...

I'm back!
I DON'T WANT TO RELY ON HAYASHIDA'S KINDNESS RIGHT NOW.
SLIDE

Wel-come back.
IT'S BAD ENOUGH
Wel-come home.
CHOP
CHOP
CHOP
Want some water-melon?
RELYING ON MY PARENTS...

Your friend was just here.
With a child...
Oh, I met them outside.
Did you, now.
Were you class-mates?
Yeah, middle school.
Huh...
AND BUMMING OFF OF THEM.

THP
THP
THP
Speaking of, do you remember our neighbor Toyokawa? You went to grade school with her.

I happened to run into her the other day. She said she's working as a nurse now.
She's still single.
GACHAK
Oh, and her sister Akko is in childcare.

Want to try a cooking class or something? Your back is mostly healed, right?
Also ... your uncle was talking about a job—
I'm taking a bath.

MY PARENTS ARE TRYING TO BE CONSIDERATE, TOO.

I'M SURE THAT IT DOESN'T TAKE LONG FOR RUMORS TO START FLYING AROUND IN THIS SMALL RURAL TOWN IF I'M HERE AT HOME, UNMARRIED AND JOBLESS.

BUT THEY'RE ACTING LIKE NOTHING IS WRONG.

EVEN THOUGH NOT HAVING GRAND-KIDS PROBABLY PUTS THEM IN THE MINORITY AT THEIR AGE.

I wonder how they feel when their friends talk about their kids and grandkids...
ZHAAAAAA

FLASH
FLASH

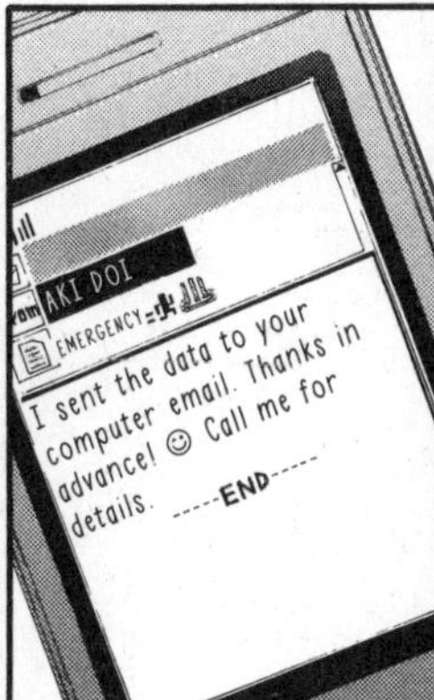
AKI DOI
EMERGENCY
I sent the data to your computer email. Thanks in advance! ☺ Call me for details. -----END-----

Aah ...
This is gonna take some time ...

Oh.
It's work.
PKAK

Hello? Aki?

Ah, Fuji-moto! You see my email?
Omu-sensei has specific instruc-tions so I'll put him on.

Hello?
I really need you to take this aerial shot of Tokyo and make it so no one can tell what the original photo was.
Okay!
Ah!
Okay, Put Screen-tone on that!
Okay.
I'M WORKING PART-TIME NOW AS A DIGITAL BACKGROUND ASSISTANT FOR OMU-SENSEI.
WELL, IT'S MORE LIKE HE HIRED ME BECAUSE HE'S LOOKING OUT FOR ME.
My deadline is tonight, so can you hurry?

Okay, thank you!
So, how're you doing?
Huh, that's great!
AKI DOI IS STILL WORKING AS OMU-SENSEI'S MANAGER.

Sounds like you won't be able to make this year's Fuji Rock, then.
Let's go together next year! I promise it'll be fine!!

You don't need to worry about me,
so just focus on healing up.
AAH...
Maybe I'll go out there to have some fun once I can take time off! Show me around!
'bye!

Bip
...
SHE MIGHT ONLY BE DATING ME RIGHT NOW BECAUSE IT'D BE TOO AWKWARD TO REJECT ME WHILE I'M INJURED.
ACTUALLY, WE'RE BARELY DATING RIGHT NOW, ANYWAY, SINCE WE CAN'T MEET UP (AND IN FACT I HAVEN'T EVEN TOLD HER HOW I FEEL YET).
She's really ...
looking out for me...
whew
BUT I CAN'T DO ANYTHING AT THE MOMENT...
IT FEELS LIKE SHE DOESN'T LOVE ME, BUT THAT SHE'S JUST TRYING TO BE CONSIDERATE TOWARDS ME.

IT WAS LIKE MY LIFE WENT OVER A CLIFF AT 30 WHEN I SAID GOODBYE TO OVER TEN YEARS OF LIVING IN TOKYO.
WHOOAAAAA うぉぉぉ
AAAA おお

BUT, WELL, IT'S NOT AS IF THE FALL KILLED ME.
Huh?
It hurt, but I'm alive.
You can do it!
But you don't have to try too hard!
EVERYONE'S BEING NICE AND CHEERING ME ON, TOO.
It's just about getting in the right mindset!
But don't push yourself too hard!

NOW THAT I'M AT THE BOTTOM, I JUST HAVE TO CRAWL MY WAY BACK UP.
Ugh, this sucks... I wanna give up...
Ugh, staying here does suck... I might as well climb up...
I FEEL AT EASE BECAUSE IT'S CLEAR WHAT I HAVE TO DO, BUT I STILL FEEL A BIT ANXIOUS BECAUSE I CAN'T SEE THE PATH AHEAD.

I'm letting myself be hurt and frustrated by the kindness of others.
I've got too much time to think about stupid stuff...
Shit...

AM I JUST GOING TO SIT HERE
UNDER THIS ROOF
AND SLOWLY ROT TO DEATH?

Yukiyo!
Can I come in?
NOK
NOK
NOK
NOK
NOK
NOK
Again...?

SLIDE
What?
Take a look at this.

Huh ?

How'd you figure out I was back, Fuji?

Oh ...

Sorry for not letting you know.

I didn't want to worry you, Fuji.

You don't need to come if your back still hurts.

I'll go over and say hi once I'm done...

We're friends! C'mon, don't be such a stranger! you should've called me!!

What are you mad about?

Agh... Sorry. I have to finish work before I can go ...
I might not make it to the wake...
I got a re-quest!
We're staying at the funeral home, so you can show up at any hour. I'll be waiting for you. Let's both do our best!!
Ack... Sorry ...
Eek!
I didn't make it in time for the wake...
WHRRR
Ah!
Fuji!
Sorry I'm so late.
You coulda just come to the service.
No, no ...
I wanted to get here earlier ...
HM?
IS IT JUST ME, OR DOES SHIMADA LOOK PRETTY WORN OUT?
Thanks, Fuji.
You should go see grand-pa.

Grand-pa Kinzo ...
I can't believe he ate some mochi when we weren't looking and got it stuck in his throat ...
ZZZZ
It's almost hard to cry about it.
mnch mnch
Ninety-six, though. And he went peace-fully.
Ah!
Have some sushi, Fujimoto !!
...

HM?

Let's drink, Fuji!!
Funerals in our family are always like this!
Grandpa never liked sad, quiet scenes anyway !
Ah, uh, OK.
Uh, cheer —
Er, thank you.

Shi-ma-da.
By the way, where's your wife?
Oh, Yurie?

She caught a cold and can't get out of bed, so I came alone.
Huh...
She really wanted to be here, though.
Grandpa liked her, so she wanted to see him one last time.

It's too bad. I haven't seen her since the wedding.
Then come up to Tokyo some time, Auntie Kazuko!
Really? Can I?
Sure!
I bought a bunch of guest futons because I assumed everyone'd start showing up, ha ha! You wanted to visit anyway, right?
Yurie looks forward to it, too!

Still no kids, Yuichi?
Not yet! I do want one soon, but we're just so busy with stuff...
We've got a big family, so I'm sure someone can help out!!
...
Oh.
Sorry, let me run to the bath-room.

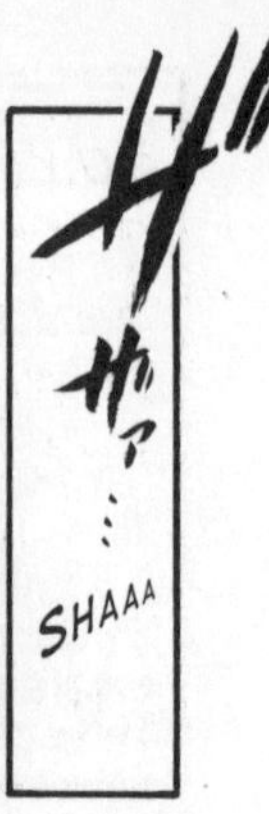
ザァ…
SHAAA

Ur... p...
...gh...
Bleh...

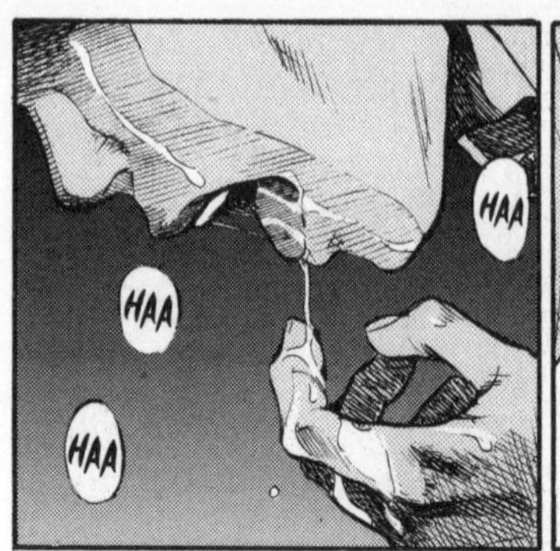
HAA
HAA
HAA

BANG
BANG
BANG
BANG
Hey.
Shimada.

Are you okay? Did you just puke?
Hey...!
Shima-da!
BANG
BANG
BANG
BANG
BANG
BANG

GACHAK
Ah!

SHAAAA
Ah, sorry. I'm fine.
SPLSH
SPLSH

I feel better now that I puked.
Let's go back and drink some more.
KACHAK
KATT
KATT
...

Some-thing happened, didn't it?
RECEPTION
You're acting weird, Shima-da.

You used to never talk about wanting kids.
You always said you didn't need them yet, right?
Why're you lying like that?
You're acting really weird, being so careful around every-one.

You don't need to be con-siderate with me.
It's gross to see you act this way.
Just tell me!!
C'mon!

I...

might be getting divorced.

... Huh ?
PARDON?
Yurie went back to her parents' house three months ago.
I lied about her being sick.
Wh... Whaa ?
But when I saw you before I moved home, you two were so...
we'll be visiting home soon!
It was already getting tricky then. We were just acting for everyone else's sake.

I've already apologized again and again, but Yurie doesn't want to talk any-more.
She told me she wants to get officially divorced.
But... how can that happen?
You two just got married last year... and you two were getting along so well.
Why would Yurie...
OH.
HUH?
COULD IT BE...
...
Yeah.
Well...
NO, DON'T TELL ME THAT YOU...
I cheated on her.

Is that really the kind of person you are ?!
Are you stupid or something ?!
Why would you do that ...?
You're the worst!
...
Why would you go to another woman after getting married to someone as beautiful as Yurie?
It doesn't make sense! It's such a waste!
If you're gonna get married, then ...
You wouldn't understand, Fuji!

YOU WOULDN'T UNDERSTAND,
FUJI.

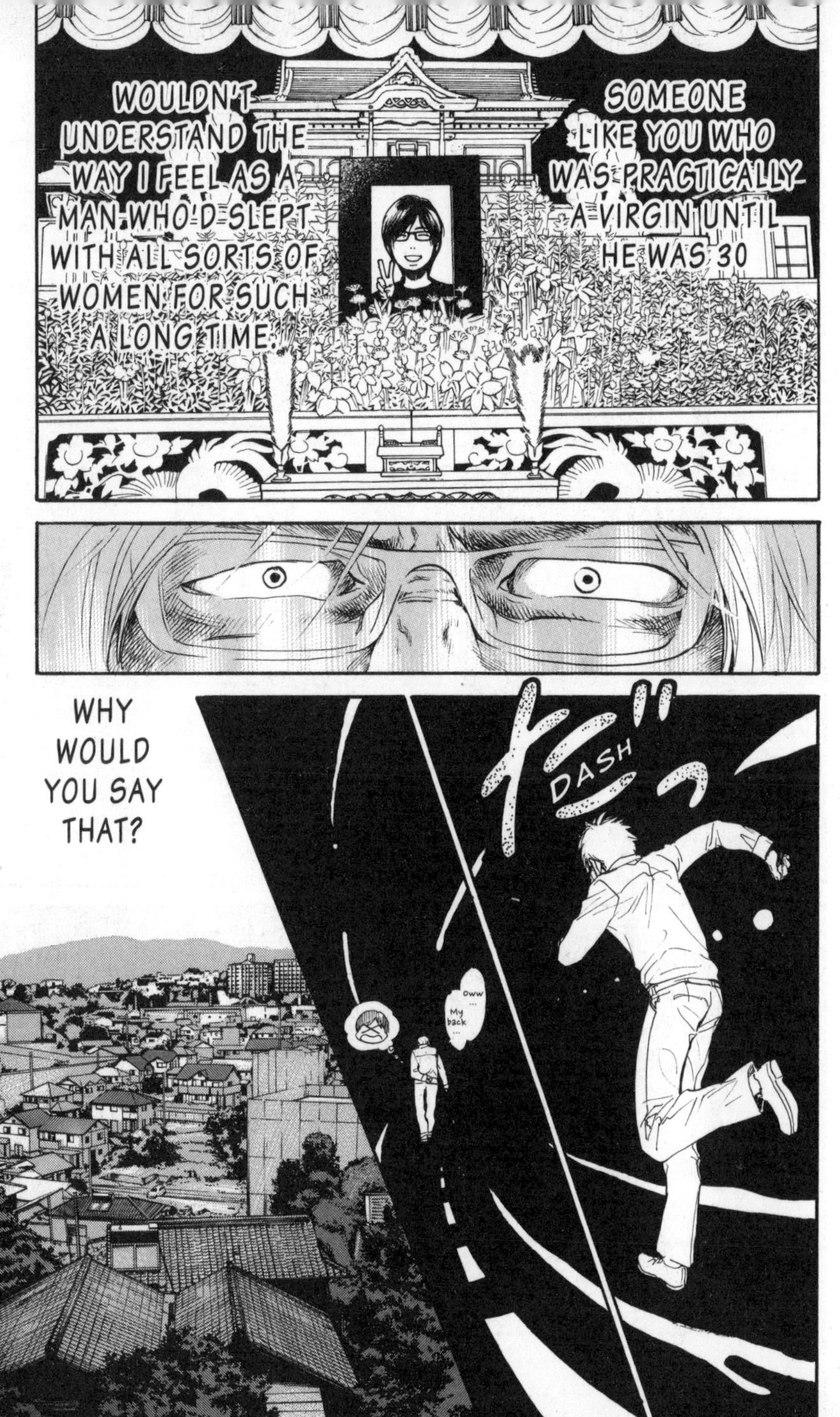
SOMEONE LIKE YOU WHO WAS PRACTICALLY A VIRGIN UNTIL HE WAS 30
WOULDN'T UNDERSTAND THE WAY I FEEL AS A MAN WHO'D SLEPT WITH ALL SORTS OF WOMEN FOR SUCH A LONG TIME.
WHY WOULD YOU SAY THAT?
DASH
Oww... My back...

Oh.
Are you not going to the service, Yukiyo?
I'm not!
I'm going for a walk!
...
KLIK
KLIK
KLIK

MAYBE... IT WAS SOME SMALL INFIDELITY.
IT COULD BE THAT YURIE CAN'T BRING HERSELF TO BACK DOWN. SHE'S STRONG-WILLED.
DIALING
SHIMADA'S WIFE
XXXXXXXXX
WHAT REALLY HAPPENED ?!

GA-CHIK
... Yes?
Oh, hello? Yurie? It's me, it's Fujimoto! It's nice to talk to you again!
...What is it? Yu must have asked you to call, right?
No! Not at all! In fact, I'm on your side!
... Did he cheat on you?
Did he really ...?
...

Unh ...
I... I just can't believe him...
WHIIINE
FRRNGH
FRRNGH
I looked through every one of the texts and calls on Yu's phone... And then when I started going down and contacting all of them... they all said they were dating...! Hic!

"All of them"...? So does that mean ...

It wasn't just one! There were a bunch!!

Ex-girlfriends, coworkers, women he met on the train, women he met at bars, he was cheating with all of them!!

SO MY OLD PARTNER IN VIRGINITY
HAD ALREADY REACHED
SUCH DISTANT HEIGHTS ?!
SHIMADA
No way ...

It's true !!
Did you not know anything, Fujimoto ?
No ...
I just heard a little yesterday... but nothing about the number of women or anything ...
Really ?

You know that one of your friends

was one ...

What do you mean... my friend?

"Natsuki."
MREEEN
TRILLLL
TRILLLL
MREEN
MREEN
I talked to a woman that was in his phone as "Natsuki."
MREEEN
MREEN
MREEN
Three months ago.

chapter 26 ♥ Shooting Star Bebop

You knew about that Natsuki woman, didn't you, Fujimoto ?!
PANT
PANT
PANT
PANT
FRRNGH
FRRNGH
You just kept it a secret from me because you're her friend!

You knew that Yu was cheating on me, didn't you?
Even before we got married !!

I DIDN'T KNOW
ARE YOU IN LOVE?
THAT HE WAS CHEATING ON HER WITH NATSUKI KOMI-YAMA,
THAT SHIMADA IS STILL SEEING HER...
I CHEATED ON HER.
I DIDN'T KNOW ABOUT ANY OF IT, I DIDN'T HEAR ABOUT IT, AND I DON'T UNDERSTAND IT.

Come on, Fujimoto! Say some-thing!!
Uh!
GASP
Ah... No, I didn't ...
You're trying to cover for Yu because you're his friend, right?!

No, I'm not trying to cover for him... I really just learned about this for the first time yesterday ...
All he told me was that he was prob-ably get-ting divorced because he'd cheated...
DRIP
I didn't realize any-thing about what kinds of women he was seeing...
DRIP
DRIP

... ...
You're his friend but you didn't know anything ?
URGH?!
Really ?

Uh ...
I really was shocked ever since I heard yesterday ...
That's why I'm calling you like this, Yurie...
Urh ...
Ah... Unhh ...
PSHAP
Ah ...
I'm sorry. So Yu was hiding it from you, too.

I'd had a vague feeling he was seeing other women even before we got married.
He's so kind to everyone, both men and women.
But I thought I'd overlook it so long as I didn't find out the details.
I was hoping he'd change after marriage ...

But even after we were married, he'd often stay out all night, and he would talk about how he doesn't want kids yet...
He just wouldn't say anything to me.
I can't believe you! It's Christmas...
BAM
I'M SORRY!!
We fought a lot,
but in the end, it was always just me getting mad at him. He'd only apologize and wouldn't try to make excuses.

It made me wonder if I wasn't satisfying him somehow... I felt so lonely.
I mean... I love Yu, after all...
Ah ...
I see ...
Uhm... So what I wanted to ask was...
And then three months ago, I found it!
The other phone he used for his women!!
ISN'T THAT TERRIBLE ?!
?!
I FOUND IT ONE NIGHT WHEN HE CAME HOME DRUNK.
SNOORE
Zzz

WHEN I LOOKED AT THE CALL HISTORY AND THE MESSAGES ON IT, HE WAS TALKING TO WAY MORE WOMEN THAN I COULD'VE IMAGINED.

Wake up, Yu!!

What is this phone?!

ZNOOORE

Hey, wake up! You need to explain this to me!!

GRR

I COULDN'T STOP MYSELF AFTER THAT.

KLIK

KLIK

KLIK

TRILLL...

TRILLL...

Who is this? What do you do?

What's your relationship to my husband?!

Don't play dumb!

I'm Shimada's wife!!

I don't want you ever seeing him again!

THEY ALL ADMITTED TO HAVING RELATIONSHIPS WITH YU...

Hello?

Who is this?!

CALLING

00:00:04

NATSUKI

EXCEPT FOR ONE.

Oh... Oh!! Yurie, right?! Shimada's wife! Good evening!

You don't need to worry about me at all! Ha ha ha ha ha! Oh, sorry for laughing.

We haven't done anything yet.

He and I are friends.

Yeah, just friends.

SNOOORE

YURIE... I LOVE YOU...!

Z Z Z

Shimada just yelled that he loves you. Why not trust him?

THEY HAVEN'T DONE ANYTHING ?!
JUST FRIENDS ?!
WHAT'S THAT SUPPOSED TO MEAN? I UNDER-STAND THAT LESS THAN ACTUALLY CHEATING!!
Shit ...
TRILLL
TRILLL
So who is this "Natsuki" person ?
Looking at their texts, it seems like they met up all the time...
Yu said that he hadn't done anything with her because she was your friend, but I just can't believe him anymore...
whiiine
whiiine
Damn it, Fuji. Why're you ignoring my calls ...?
Yu ...!

Yu!
Hiro and the other kids seem bored. Come over and play with them!
Hey, Yu!
Sure...
I'll be right over.
PTAK

vvt
vvt
vvt
vvt
vvt
vvt
vvt
vvt
?!
KPOP
KLIK
NATSUKI
Re:
Ah ...
... Oh, it's just her ...

What is this monster ...?
...

"Where am I right now?" ... What?
MUTTER
Oh!
That's Tu-Tu!
Oh, it really is! I met Tu-Tu just the other day!

You know this?
Yep!
Tu-Tu is in Big Holland Village!
Tu-Tu's the child of a tulip and an octopus!
I go there with Mom all the time!

Oh!
This thing!!
I was playing with this just a second ago.

Big Holland Village...? You mean the huge resort in this prefecture...?
I haven't been there in ages ...
... Wait, huh ?!
Then that means ...

She ...
really showed up. I can't believe her.

MREEN
MREEN
MREEN
MREEN

Ack... I have voicemail...
A text, too...
It has to be Shimada. What does he want?
IS HE PLANNING TO TELL ME ABOUT SEEING NATSUKI KOMIYAMA?
HOW AM I SUPPOSED TO REACT TO THAT?
HAVE THOSE TWO NOT HAD SEX YET BECAUSE THEY'RE JUST FRIENDS? OR HAVE THEY DONE IT ALREADY?
WHEN SHE SAID THERE'S SOMEONE SHE LIKES, DID SHE MEAN SHIMADA?
BUT SHE SAID IT WAS SOMEONE I DIDN'T KNOW!!
WHY WOULD SHE DECIDE TO GO AFTER SHIMADA?
WAIT, WHO MADE THE FIRST MOVE, ANYWAY?

I DON'T WANT TO KNOW.
SNAP
It's been a while
since I've walked this way.
SHIMADA AND I WENT TO MIDDLE AND HIGH SCHOOL TOGETHER, BUT WE WEREN'T ALL THAT CLOSE AS FRIENDS.

WE HAD TOTALLY DIFFERENT TASTES IN MANGA AND MUSIC,
BUT BACK THEN, WE DIDN'T HAVE CERTAIN CONDITIONS FOR PEOPLE TO BECOME FRIENDS.
...
KPOP
You know... he was always thinking about grandpa Kinzo.
They'd always been close, and Shimada came home all the time when his grandpa was hospitalized.
I thought the shock of losing him was what had caused Shimada to look so emaciated at first.
This is a really tough time for Shimada, the cheating included, but I haven't done a thing for him.

BADUM
BEEP
BEEP
Aah!
It really is you, Fuji-moto!
LUCKY
I heard you'd come back and I wanted to see you!
Oh, hello!
THP
Oh... (Buru-ko).
Come with us to grab some-thing to eat!!

I GUESS I CAN TALK TO HIM LATER.
Danger Hut
とんかつ
HAHAKATSU

Kishi-kawa is balding now? For real?!
He is, he is! I saw him at the reunion the other day!! Says he hasn't gotten married yet.
Well it'd be hard...
And he used to look so cool! I was shocked.
GRIND
GRIND
Did you know those two were dating in high school?
Oh, I knew. It was totally obvious.

Did you know, Fuji-moto?
Oh...
Yeah, I think I remember them dating...
AH! SO IT'S TRUE!!
GRIND
GRIND

You all know so much about what happened in high school... even upper-classmen.
Oh, people had been talking about it a lot online lately!
GRIND
GRIND
I talk to my club seniors a lot, too.
Oh, that's right!
Sesame seeds to mix with the pork cutlet sauce
GRIND

Fujimoto, do you know who Sakurako Kanzaki is?
GRRK

MY FIRST LOVE, SAKURAKO. THE GIRL WHO REJECTED ME AFTER I TOLD HER I LIKED HER...
Sorry ...
Oh ...
I guess ...

Wasn't she famous or something? For doing it with everyone at school?
People were really freaking out over that on the Mixi group recently!
I didn't know about her since she was four years ahead of us...
Oh... Sounds like it ...
what a shock, right?
Ah! I heard the same about my senior on the soccer team!
I can't believe they could do that!
GRIND
I DIDN'T KNOW AT THE TIME, BUT SHE'D HAVE SEX IN THE EMPTY ROOM NEXT DOOR... YEP, UH-HUH.
did it with a bunch of guys in an empty classroom
Next door didn't notice

I was shocked when I heard she even did it with Shimada!
Right ?
GRIN
GRIN

GR...

...WHUT?!
Huh?
You knew about that, right?
Ah...
Uhh...
I don't really... know the details...
Wh... What?
Didn't Shimada ever tell you?
I saw it when I was a sophomore.
That Sakurako Kanzaki girl had come to school.
Apparently she was back from college for summer break or something.
Who is that woman...?
Handmade cookies
Sakurako!
It's been so long! Do you remember me?
Oh, Fujimoto's friend on the baseball team?
Hey!
College out for summer?
Shimada was the one who called out to her.
RADIO CLUB
After chatting for a bit...

LITERATURE CLUB

SLIDE PSHAP

they went into that room she used for hook-ups.

...

THP THP THP THP

スタスタスタスタ…

FUJIMOTO!

Uhm ...

Please eat these handmade cookies!

Do you ever shut up, Miss Ugly...?

SHAKA SHAKA SHAKA SHAKA

SLIDE

WAH HA HA

PSHAP

DID HE ACTUALLY HATE ME ALL THIS TIME?

Huh?
Yuki-yo's not around?
He hasn't been home since going out for his walk.
He emailed me to say that he was going to eat out for lunch.
Come in and wait here, Shimada.

...

Oh.
No thank you.
You sure?
Uhm ...
Could you give him a note from me?
Could I borrow a pen and some paper?

Thank you.
Could you take me to Big Holland Village?

Big Holland Village

TUU!
TUU!
The fire-works are start-ing!
Isn't that right, Tu-Tu?

RAAAAH

WHO
GOT-CHA!!
WHOA!
MP
THUD
AHH!
It took you forever!
I wanted to get dinner together. I'm starving now.

Don't be ridiculous...
You know it wasn't easy for me to leave, even at this hour...

Hmm ...
So? Are you alone?
Yeah ...
I invited Fuji, but I couldn't get in touch with him... Sorry...

Oh, I wonder if he still hates me...
BOOM
BOOM

Nah.
I haven't told him yet 'cause I want it to be a surprise when you see him.

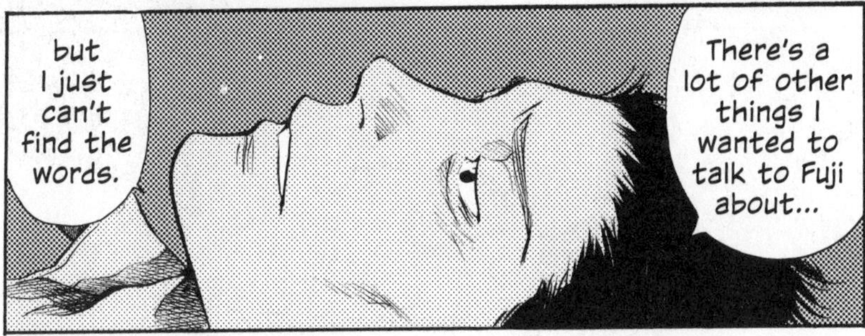
There's a lot of other things I wanted to talk to Fuji about...
but I just can't find the words.

I wanted to talk to Grandpa Kinzo about it, too,
but I didn't make it in time.
...

We'll be staying together in a hotel tonight, right?

Tell me more about your grand-dad.

I really like hearing about him.

BA

KRAKK

It'd be nice to have some wine. It's been a while.

Hm?

What, are you trying to comfort me?

Of course I am. We're friends, after all.

BA KRAKK

BOO OOM

TREMBLE
TREMBLE
Fuji-
There's something I want to talk to you about.
I'll be waiting at Big Holland Village.
Shimada

Shimada came in the evening. You should hurry up and contact him.
Look how late it is...
Yuki-yo?
THAT
PIECE OF SHIT.

WHAT MORE DOES HE WANT TO DO TO ME?!

I'M GONNA KILL YOU IF THIS IS ALL TRUE,

SHIMADAAA!

BOOM

BOOM

BOOM

DASH

M o t e k i   M i t s u r o u   K u b o

M o t e k i

M i t s u r o u   K u b o

chapter 27 ♥ Summer Nude

Shi-
mada.

Did
you
really
sleep
with
them
...?

Uh, you
know...

With
Sakura-
ko...

And
with
Na-
tsuki
Komi-
yama
...

...

I'm
sor-
ry!

KAPOW

YOU
DUMB-
ASS
!!

Being a man means being ready to put your life on the line to protect the one and only woman you truly love, doesn't it?!

Urgh...

What're you doing, chasing one tail after another just 'cause you wanna get off?!

Hey ...

Are you listening, Yukiyo ?

I need to talk to someone man-to-man!! Please, can you drive me?!

I've already had a beer, I can't drive now.

I don't know what the story is, but you oughta calm down and tell him tomorrow!!

If you've got the energy to wander around all day long, why don't you hurry up and find a job?!

I've been meaning to say that!

GRR

ムッカー…

YUKI-YO !

Hey, listen to me !

YUKIYO!

ドス STOMP

ドス STOMP

ドス STOMP

ドス STOMP

BOOOM
BOOOM

BOOOM
The sound of fireworks coming from Big Holland Village...
I wonder if Shimada's still there.

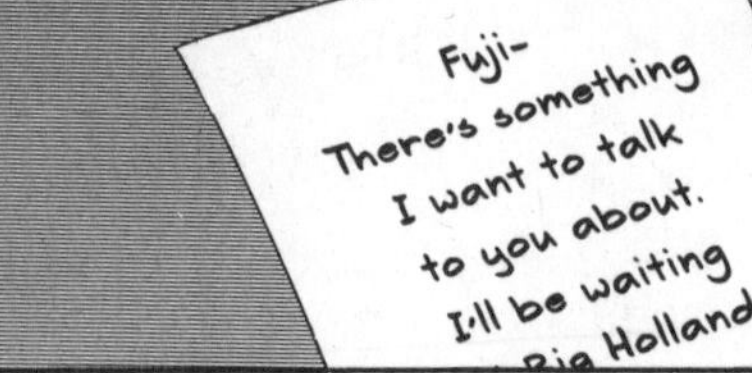

Fuji-
There's something I want to talk to you about. I'll be waiting
Big Holland

WHAT DOES HE NEED TO TELL ME?!

Whether it's debating him or fighting him, I don't have any confidence!!

WOULD I REALLY BE ABLE TO GET MAD AT SHIMADA IF I SAW HIM AND HE SAID EVERYTHING WAS TRUE? I'VE NEVER HIT SOMEONE THEN LECTURED THEM BEFORE. I FEEL LIKE I MIGHT LOSE IF HE DECIDES TO STAND UP FOR HIMSELF...

I'VE NEVER GOTTEN IN A REAL FIGHT WITH SHIMADA BEFORE.
WE'VE NEVER EVEN HAD MUCH OF A SERIOUS DISCUSSION.

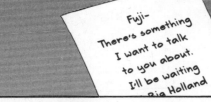

BOOOM
BOOOM
BOOOM
Yukiyo isn't coming.
Maybe we should start drinking without him?
Yeah.
I'll open the wine.
Yaay!

So, did you tell Yukiyo you were seeing other women?

I didn't give him the details, but he might've talked to Yurie about it, too.

What're you gonna do? Get a divorce?

Hmm...

I'm thinking I'd like to start over with Yurie.

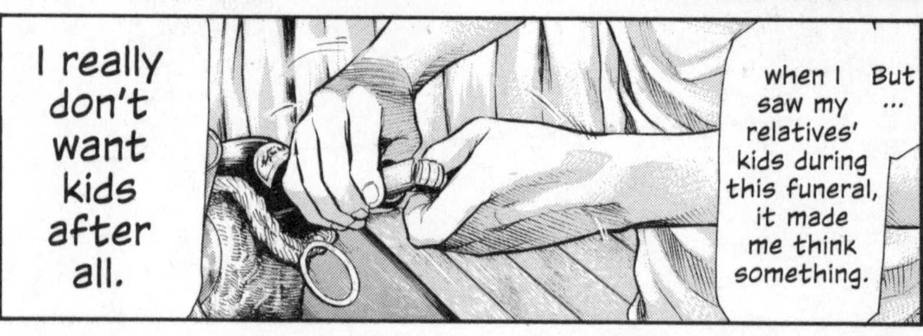

But...
when I saw my relatives' kids during this funeral, it made me think something.
I really don't want kids after all.

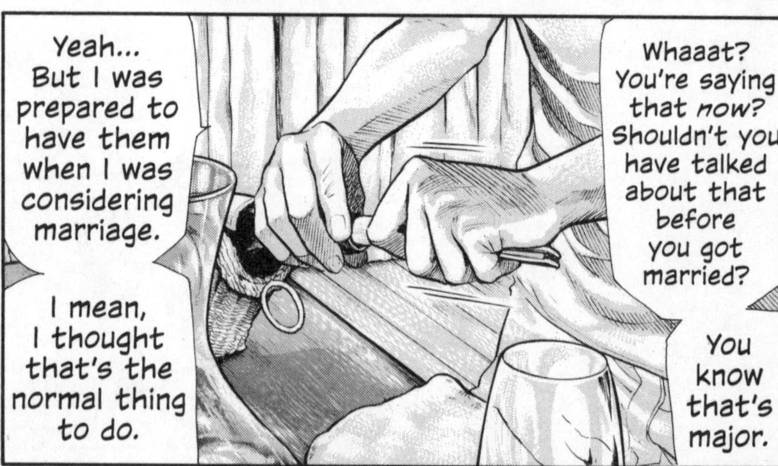

Whaaat? You're saying that *now*? Shouldn't you have talked about that before you got married?
You know that's major.
Yeah... But I was prepared to have them when I was considering marriage.
I mean, I thought that's the normal thing to do.

Now that I'm 30, I'm not sure anymore if it's okay for me to keep living this way.
I bet
Yukiyo would be pissed if he heard you say that.
"Why are you so dissatisfied?! Shimada, you came out a winner in life!!"
"You dated all kinds of girls, went to college and got a full-time job, and then married a beautiful lady!!"
"What more could you possibly want, you damn normie!!"
Like that.
I've never been able to talk to Fuji about this.

I can taste some *gloomy*, young sedi-ment ...
Like if Yukiyo had been born in Burgundy.
NOT LIKE I'D BE POPULAR IN FRANCE, EITHER! C'EST BON JE T'AIME!
SIGH
Don't worry, I'll decant it in a second.

You always wanted to try an old, expensive wine, right?
Yeah.
Huh... So this is what it tastes like... Is this all that differ-ent...?

Don't drink too much, okay?
Sure.

I'll be okay as long as you're here, Shimada.
That's why I came here to see Yukiyo like this, right?
Huh ...
So I'm here to play the stopper once again ?
My fate was sealed the night we met ...
1 year ago
ガヤ CHATTER
ガヤ CHATTER
Lemme use the bath-room ...
WOBBLE
Oh, there was an annoying couple over there just now! Go punch 'em !!
They were soooo gross !
BANG
GACHIK
SMAK
MMH...
SMAK
MMH
Yeah? After this ...
What ...?
Oh, this ...?
Excuuuse me!
Could you move ? I'm about to shit my-self!

Ah ...
Save me... Shi-mada.
What're you doing?! You seemed completely in the mood to do it!
Nooo...! He was just a guy friend.
Then tell him no! IDIOT!
Aren't you the one who hits on guys when you're drunk?
You know, like the time with me?
GRRR
Why does everyone always say that ...?
Agh! No, don't cry. When girls cry, I...
What should I do ...
I missed the last train ...
You're drunk, aren't you ?!

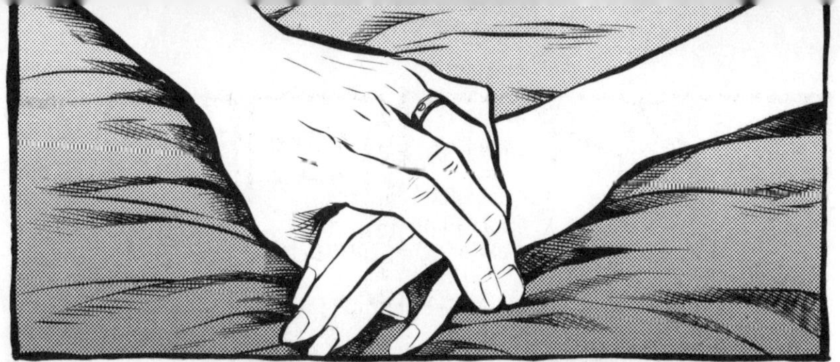

You don't want to do it?
I already told you, it's not happen-ing.
I'm married, after all.
And I can't put my hands on a friend.

You know... I used to do it with my guy friends.
Not that I have any now.
HOW DUMB ARE YOU?!
That's why you can't make friends!
Then will you be my friend?
Huh?
Why me? I'd rather die than be some-one's fuck buddy.
I just wanted a guy friend, not a lover.
It's not like I particularly like sex or any-thing.
Still no?

In that case,
would you see Fuji one more time?
As a friend.

He was traumatized by his experience with you. He can't trust women at all now.
He sees you as some kind of incomprehensible monster of a woman.

Just treat Fuji as a regular friend.
A friend he can tell anything, and one he doesn't get his hopes up for.
...

If you're with Fuji, I'll hang out with you as a friend, too.
He's not going to try to sweet-talk you into bed any-more.
Okay?
Oh, and meet him sober.

Yeah.
I *have* been feeling bad about what happened...

Sorry.
We went to a hotel.
Didn't I tell you not to drink?!
cut her hair

[SEE VOLUME 1.]

You need to learn how to handle your liquor.
I'm not gonna help if you make another misstep with a guy!
Agh... Fuji's gotta be feeling blue...
Yukiyo said he was having good luck with girls lately.
I THINK HE'LL BE FINE.
We didn't do it, though. Yukiyo couldn't get it up.
That's even worse!
LET'S DRIIINK!
I NEED TO BE HOME BY DINNER OR YURIE WILL GET MAD AT ME. JUST ONE DRINK, OKAY?
Ever since then,
it's been so easy to be around you, Shimada.
I can lean on you without you getting the wrong idea, and you never try to figure out exactly how I feel about you.
...
It's so nice to have a guy friend.

...
I can see your panties. Put those away.
Yeah. I'm showing them to you.
Listen... Like I've told you again and again, I'm not interested in you like that. You're just a friend to me.

Are you actually gay, Shimada?
You're in a sham marriage, aren't you?
BADUM BADUM
I've always loved women very much!
Like Kashimura if this was "Kosaku Shima."
I don't get that reference!!

That's what I thought. You wouldn't have cheated on your wife with so many women otherwise.
How many were you up to?
...Seven, I think.
I want you to know that they made the first move every time, okay?!
I was just treating them like friends!
I never made any advances on them!

We're friends, right?
You're an important friend to me!
I'm gonna get married soon!
You should come, you're my friend !!
Let's be buddies !!
Yeah, friends are great !!
I wonder if I was doing something weird ...
It's probably because you seemed like you wouldn't.
But I know.
Everyone suspects it, Shimada,
that normal guys like you are always gonna cheat.
They probably just wanted to see how far they could push you before you dropped the "friend" act.
...
Are you trying to push me, too?
Hmm ?

I generally don't like people who like me.
So what I like about you is the way that you don't care either way about me.

You know...
you really are like her.
Fuji's first love...
Our senior, Sakurako.
Huh...
What was she like?

Can we do it, Natsuki?
It's fine with me.

ROLL
ACK!
SHFF

OWWW...
I brought a Bordeaux, too. Why don't we open it up?
And I have some smoked duck.

I BET FUJI

ooh!

FINDS THIS KIND OF THING MYSTERIOUS AND ALLURING.

I wanna try some...

Please, Fuji! You need to learn!!

You just aren't able to handle this type of woman!!

THE MOMENT YOU GET SERIOUS WITH HER IS WHEN YOU LOSE.

AH!

...
...
KPOP
JOLT
Sub
Sorry for not getting back to you yesterday.
Are you still in Big Holland Village?
I can be there at around noon.
Fuji ...
BA-DUM

I'm cold ...

Oh!
Sorry, sorry
Are you still feeling the wine?
No, I'm fine.

Did Yukiyo con-tact you?
Oh... Yeah. He said he could be here at noon.

In that case ...
we have until noon.
What should we do?

I'M SORRY.

HAAH
I DECIDED
HAAH
HAAH
I WASN'T GOING TO DO THIS ANY-MORE.
We're gonna be late meet-ing him.
Hey ...
I think we should get going ...

HAAH
HAAH
HAAH
HAAH
Shi-ma-da?

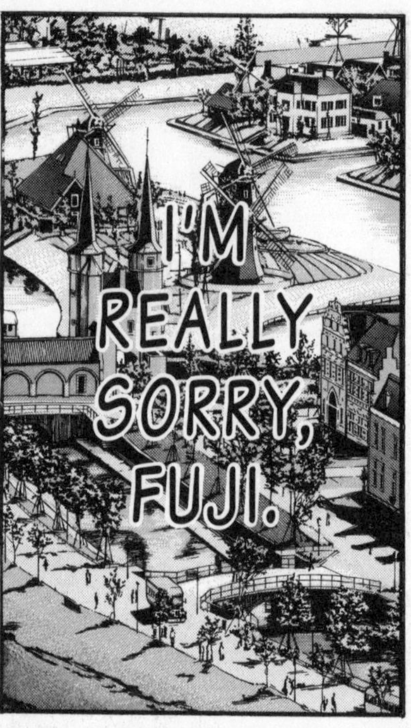
I'M REALLY SORRY, FUJI.

I DIDN'T ASK YOU TO COME HERE BECAUSE I WANTED TO DO THIS TO YOU.

Where's the ferry terminal?

CHUMS

Over there?

IF ONLY
YOU'D MET UP WITH US YESTERDAY.
IF ONLY ...

Fuji !!
Oh!
Hey !

Hm ?
Did you leave already ?
I wanted to make an appearance like a female Kosaku Shima character or something!
Hey !

chapter 27 ♥ END

chapter 28 ♥ Black Tea Love

ザザ..
ZHAAA

THEE CROUH

Nice weath-er.

Huh?

Uh, yeah.

The breeze is great, too.

It's been a while since I've been on a boat.

I bet you haven't been to Big Holland Village in ages, huh...?

Thanks for coming way out here.

Ah, it's fine.

OOH

SCRTCH SCRTCH

...

AHAHAHAHA

ZHAAA

WIPE WIPE

If he learns that I just had marathon sex with Natsuki Komiyama ...
Fuji might just die.
I could see him trying to jump into the ocean ...
HMM
I'd just look even more pathetic if I yelled at him ...
He probably came here to apologize. So I guess I'll just...

So you've never been on this boat tour before, Fuji?
Oh ...
Nope. I haven't been to this place since the time it opened.
Oh, I see!

I might've come earlier if I ever had a girlfriend, though.
AH HA! OMG, RIGHT?!
What about you, Shimada?
JOLT
Ah?
Uhm.

......
what's the matter with you today ...?
Oh.

Over there.
You can climb up to the prow.
Looks fun! Let's go!!
C'mon, Shimada!!
Huh?
No way, not me! I'm afraid of heights!!
It'll be fine! C'mon!
NOO-OOO!
OH...
HEY, SHIMADA...
DO YOU REMEMBER WHEN WE FIRST MET?
WE WERE IN THE SAME CLASS, BUT WE WEREN'T ACTUALLY FRIENDS OR ANYTHING.
I THINK IT STARTED WHEN WE WERE EATING LUNCH NEXT TO EACH OTHER AND JUST HAPPENED TO SPLIT A PACKET OF RICE SEASONING.
BONITO FLAKE SEASONING

WHEN YOU TRIED TO GIVE ME YOUR LEFTOVER WASABI SEASONING, I DIDN'T LIKE WASABI, SO...
I'm fine.
I COLDLY SHUT YOU DOWN.
BUT AFTER YOU WENT QUIET FOR A SEC-OND...
YOU DUMPED ALL OF THE WASABI SEASONING LEFT INSIDE THE PACKAGE ONTO MY RICE.
HEEYAAAA!
WAAAAAGH!
FOR SOME REASON, I NEARLY FELT LIKE CRYING WHEN YOU DID THAT.
IT'S HARD TO EXPLAIN, BUT...
BWA HA HA HA HA
I CAN'T BELIEVE YOU, SHIMA-DAAA!
I THINK THAT WAS THE MOMENT WHEN YOU DESTROYED THE WALL THAT STOOD IN THE WAY OF US BECOMING FRIENDS.
HAVE YOU CHANGED
FROM THE PERSON YOU WERE BACK THEN?
HEY, SHIMADA,
WHY DON'T WE GO BACK TO THE WAY WE WERE THEN AND...

FUJI!
I'm coming with you...!!
HEY, SHIMADA...
YOU KNOW...

I WILL ALWAYS BE ON YOUR SIDE.

Please stop, it's danger-ous!

Please!

Watch out!!

Stop it, Fuji!

AAAA

AAA AAA

So, Fuji ...

There's some-thing I never told you ...

BADUMM

About Sakurako and Natsuki, right ...?

?!

How'd you know about that (too) ...?
I heard from Yurie and Buruko ...
She said she saw you and Sakurako go into that room.
I'm ... not mad, so ...
you'll tell me everything, right?
FUJI!
I'LL ACCEPT IT ALL.
Hey, that's risky!
Uhm...!
BECAUSE I BELIEVE IN YOU.

LIKE THIS, AND...

FLAP

FLAP

... And then
I was doing it with Natsuki until this morning.
...
...
...
...
...
...
Are you listen-ing, Fuji?
So, uhm ...
Starting with when Sakurako came back to school. So... Buruko was telling the truth?
Uuhh ...
Uhm ...
Yup.
Sorry.
I still haven't really processed everything you said and my mind is all mixed up.
THEE CROUH
Oh... I'm sure.
Oh!
Like I said, that was...

She happened to come back to school because she was home from her college in Tokyo for summer break.
I just thought... you might get hung up on her again, so...
I was trying to keep you two apart.
ZHAAA

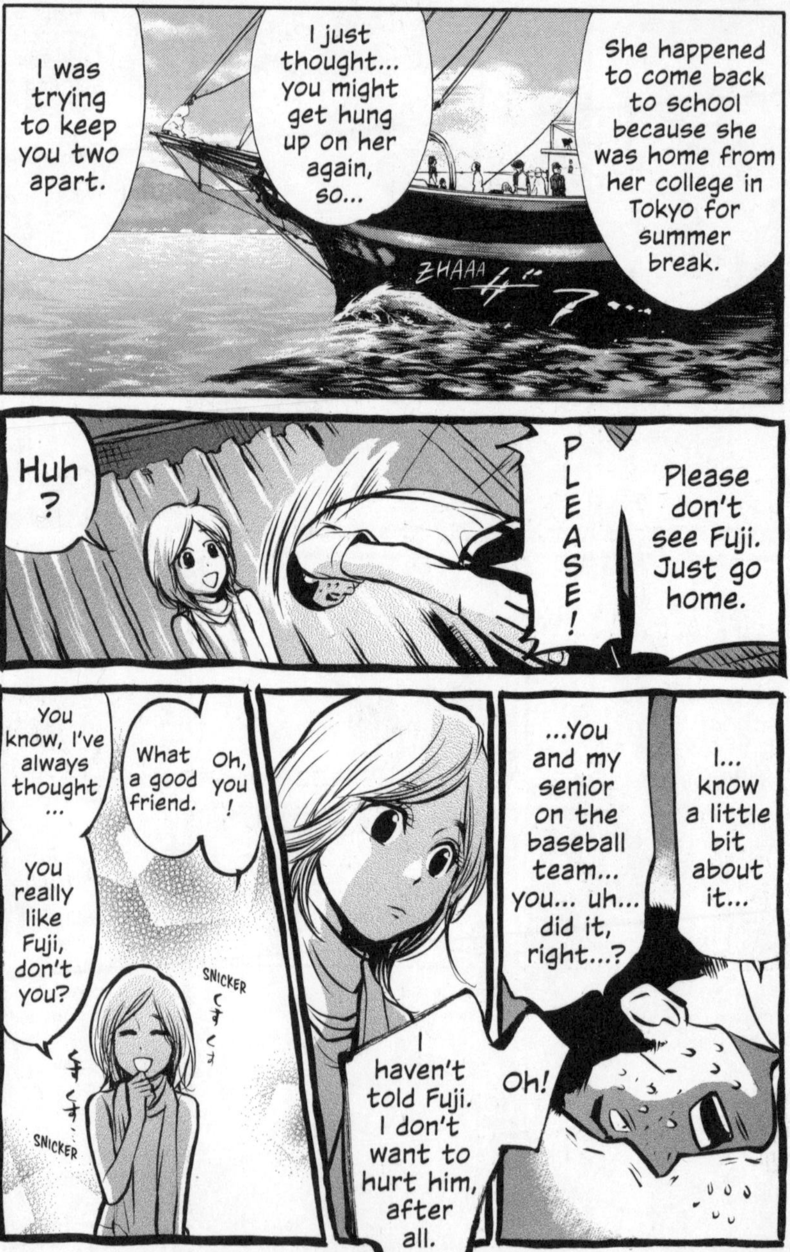

Please don't see Fuji. Just go home.

PLEASE!

Huh?

I... know a little bit about it...

...You and my senior on the baseball team... you... uh... did it, right...?

Oh!

I haven't told Fuji. I don't want to hurt him, after all.

Oh, you!

What a good friend.

You know, I've always thought...

you really like Fuji, don't you?

SNICKER

SNICKER

What school are you trying for next year, Shimada?
Huh?
Uhm... I want to go to school in Tokyo, but...
Oh!
Re-ally...!
Well, let's hold a mixer if you ever come to Tokyo.
HUH?
Really, nothing hap-pened then...!
I swear...
I never had any intentions like that until I went to school in Tokyo and saw her again at a mixer...
And I was still a virgin back then, too...
And so...
you slept with Sakurako.
And so...
you dated for a while without telling me... like you just said.
No... Listen, Fuji, I...!

We were basically just friends with benefits.

She had other guys, anyway.

We broke up because I couldn't take it any longer.

We did it when we met up, though.

I didn't have money, I wasn't all that hot... I didn't understand why she picked someone like me.

I feel like that's when it all blew up for me.

I never fooled around in high school, so it was like I was making up for lost time.

I was such an idiot...

In the end, that just made it easier for me to cheat on a woman.

The reason I tell women things like "We're just friends,"

or, "I only sleep with women I'm in love with,"

is because I feel like they're about to overwhelm me and sweep me away.

Even after I got married to Yurie,

nothing about me changed.

I've just let myself get swept along.

Aren't you in love with Natsuki,
Shimada?
...
Weren't you in love with Sakurako?
I still think...
about that last summer in high school.
Even yesterday. If only you'd come, Natsuki and I wouldn't have...
Why are you always placing the blame on other people?
THEE CROUH
I still wish that I hadn't run into Sakurako before you.

Sorry.
No, don't say sorry!
BAM
Do you know how hard I'm trying to avoid saying things like,
"My life might be different if only I'd done something different then"?
So don't you start saying it now!
"Oh, if only I'd gone into that hotel with Natsuki that night."
I don't wanna think about that!
Not about Sakurako, not about other women, not about anything!
Just let me resign myself to the thought that there was only one thing I could've done, that I had no other choice.

I have to believe that my life wouldn't change
over some-thing as small as that!
What, would my life have turned out like yours, or some-thing?
Of course not!
Shit.
What I'm trying to say is...
This is the life you chose, isn't it?!
So be proud of it!
But ...
I'm in the wrong here.
You're mad, aren't you?
Of course I am! At least give me the freedom to hate you!
For a long time now... I've always felt so pathetic every time I talk to you...
Do you think I'm stupid? Do you think I'm so mag-nanimous that I'd forgive you?!
ESPECIALLY AFTER ALL THAT EXTRA STUFF YOU JUST TOLD ME...!
GUH ...

No, I don't think you're stupid!
No, I know you were treating me like a fool!
Even if I did, I didn't think you were stupid!
I was the one being stupid, that's all!!
You were looking down on me as some kinda poor, fat, virgin geek, right?! I'm sure of it!
Agh! I knew it!!
BTT
BTT

What about you, Fuji? Can you live your life proudly?!
Huh?
You'd better not be thinking that I'm the same guy I was back in middle school!!
SFF

ZHAAAA

ZHAAAA

Wh...
Why did you bring Na-tsuki here?!
Huh?
You're still not over her, right?
What? I'm totally over her!!
I don't have anything to say to her!!
THEE

Seeing her is just going to hurt me again!
She's just here to make fun of my pathetic self, isn't she?!
No!
I don't wanna see her!
FUJI!!
YOU REALLY FOUND ME ANNOYING THIS WHOLE TIME, DIDN'T YOU, SHIMADA?

I'M NOT LIVING SO BOLDLY THAT I HAVE ANY RIGHT TO LECTURE YOU.
I'M FULL OF REGRETS ABOUT THE LIFE I'VE CHOSEN.
I WAS ALWAYS PATHETIC COMPARED TO YOU.
I DON'T KNOW THE RIGHT ANSWERS.
I...
SHOULD JUST DISAPPEAR.
YOU ALWAYS FELT THE SAME WAY, RIGHT?

SPLAAAASH
I WANT TO VANISH
AND BE GONE.

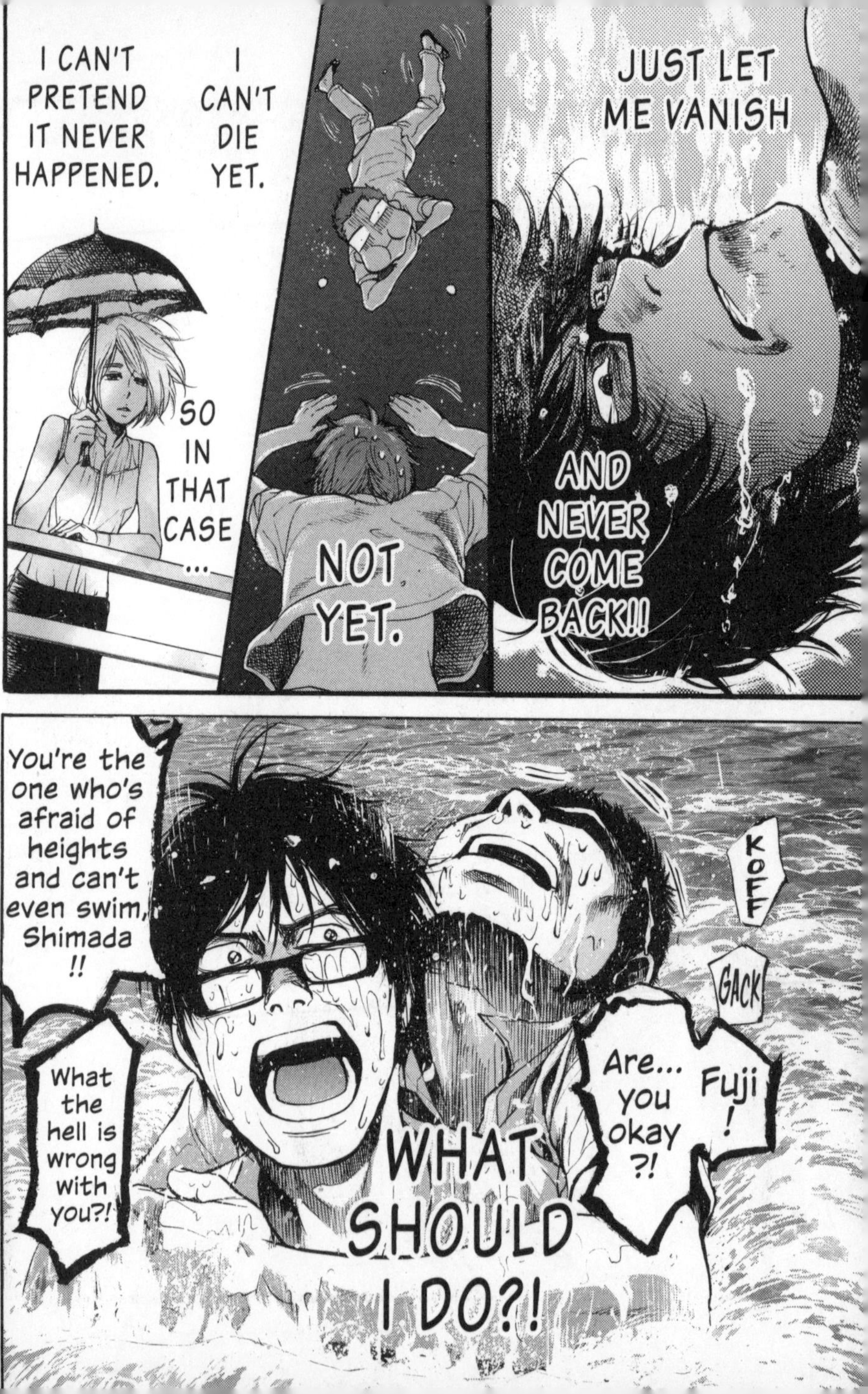

JUST LET ME VANISH

AND NEVER COME BACK!!

I CAN'T DIE YET.

NOT YET.

I CAN'T PRETEND IT NEVER HAPPENED.

SO IN THAT CASE ...

Fuji!

Are... you okay?!

KOFF

GACK

WHAT SHOULD I DO?!

You're the one who's afraid of heights and can't even swim, Shimada!!

What the hell is wrong with you?!

chapter 28 ♥ END

chapter 29 ♥ Trampoline Girl

I DIDN'T WANT TO MEET AGAIN
LIKE THIS.

DRIP
DRIP
DRIP
DRIP
I DIDN'T EVER
...

WANT TO SEE HER AGAIN.

I DIDN'T WANT TO SEE

THE WOMAN

I'VE LOVED MOST IN MY LIFE.

I was watching!
I saw you two swimming together.

I can't believe you jumped from the boat. What were you two idiots doing?
Oh, I get it...
...
You jumped into the ocean because you were hot, right?

The two of you really are super close!

AACK!
HEAVE-HO
YOU'RE TO BLAME FOR THIS, TOO!
Fuji.
I know what you're thinking right now.
For real?
I guess I shouldn't be surprised.

Isn't the weather nice today?
I should've brought a swimsuit!
I wanna go swimming!
YOU HAVE NO IDEA HOW I FEEL...
HOW CAN YOU SHOW UP ACTING SO CAREFREE?
ESPECIALLY AFTER YOU DUMPED ME.

Why do I feel so unsatisfied right now ...?
Yeah ...
Falling into the ocean cut off the chance for us to settle things between us...
Ha ha ha ha...
First things first, though, I wanna change into dry clothes ...
...
Let's go to a cafe or something! I want some iced tea!
...

I'm hopping in the shower for a sec.
I'm a friend!
Ah!
Nice to see you again! I'm Shimada!!
Oh ... That's fine.
Been a while ...

You take Natsuki back to your family's place.
Like I said, my relatives are still there ...

Thanks for letting me come in!
WHY ARE YOU EVEN CHASING ME INTO MY OWN HOME?!
TURN

IT'S SO CRAMPED. WHY IS THERE SO LITTLE SPACE IN MY HEART?

SLIIDE
Stay calm. Stay calm ...

GLUG
GLUG

WHY ARE YOU LETTING HER DRINK ?!
Huh?
You can really knock 'em back!
Ahh ~!
Mmm, that's good!

Hey, Shi-mada! Stop her, you ...
Wait, where is he ?
He had to run because he got a sudden call from his family.
He said they were going around making calls.

WHAA?!
SORRY!!

Would you like to eat some champon*, Natsuki?
Yes, please !!
WHAT AM I SUPPOSED TO DO NOW?!

*fried noodles with pork and seafood

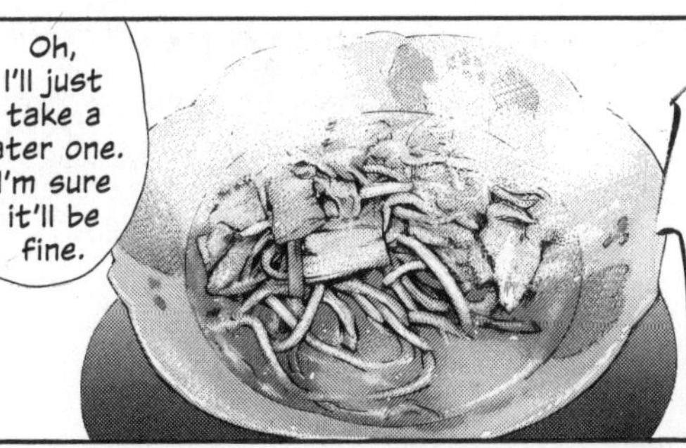

So you're flying home today? When's your flight back, Natsuki?
Oh, I'll just take a later one. I'm sure it'll be fine.

We're in rural Japan, there aren't that many flights from here!! And do you really expect to get on a flight right after drinking?!

Oh, you're going back already?
Why not stay here? You're welcome to.
What, really? Are you sure that's okay?
NO! IT'S NOT OKAY!!

I don't see what the problem is. She came all the way here from Tokyo to see you, right?

Oh, should we open some wine?

White?

We've got sashimi from that fish I caught yesterday, right?

OH, NO.

THEY'VE TOTALLY MISTAKEN HER FOR MY GIRL-FRIEND.

Mm heh heh...

I'M SORRY.

I'VE

ALREADY BEEN DUMPED BY HER.

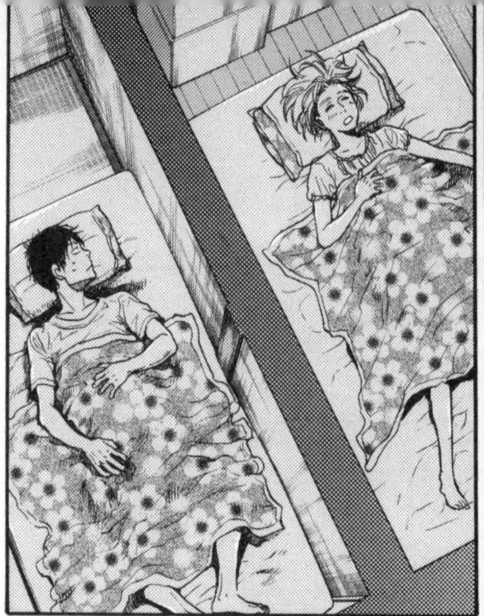

SNOOORE

To think that Natsuki Komiyama is on the other side of this wall...
It makes me wonder if she'll have disappeared by the time I wake up tomorrow... Actually, I really wish she would disappear!!

I'M JUST GLAD WE DIDN'T GET INTO ANYTHING SEX-RELATED IN FRONT OF MY PARENTS...
HA HA HA HA HA HA
BWA HA HA HA
Aw, I'm so jealous, Yukiyo!
You have such great par- ents!
BAM
BAM
You've said that a dozen times now, Natsuki ...

Oh, am I being too loud?
Oops.
No, no, it's fine.
It's fun to have such a lively dinner for once.
FLAP
FLAP
Yukiyo is such a reserved boy.

Yukiyooo! Ya know you gotta talk to your parents, riight! Communi-caaaate!!
Uh ... Uh-huh.
Did she always act this way?
You know you're really lucky to have a home to come back to when you can't work!!

I've told you this before, but I don't have any parents, and my big sister is married now...
I'm not close to any of my relatives, so I don't have anywhere to go back to! It's so much fun to have a gathering like this!
...
Aah ...
Yeah, she did tell me that before... When was it...?
What ?!
I took a trip right now because I just quit my job.
I'm so glad I came ~!!
My word! Well, please relax here!

Would it be okay for me to stay here?
Now that we finally got to meet up again, it'd be nice to sit and talk with you a little more, Yukiyo.
I think it's fate that we've been able to meet again !!
Is that how you lured Shimada in, too?!
What a total slut !!

WRITHE
WRITHE
WRITHE
WRITHE
WRITHE
She wanted to see me...? I don't understand what she's thinking at all...
Doesn't she like Shimada?
Why can't she just leave me alone?
She doesn't want to date me, does she?

SHE TELLS ME SHE CAN'T SEE ME AS A MAN...
SHE GOES TO A HOTEL WITH ME...
SHE TELLS ME SHE'S NEVER REALLY FALLEN IN LOVE WITH ANYONE...
SHE TELLS ME SHE MET SOMEONE SHE LOVES...
SHE DOESN'T MIND HELPING MY FRIEND CHEAT ON HIS WIFE...

WHICH ONE IS THE REAL NATSUKI KOMIYAMA?

VVT VVT VVT VVT VVT VVT

JOLTT

BAM
PKAK
Good...job...!
THIS IS NO TIME TO LET OTHER WOMEN TOY AROUND WITH ME.
AKI DOI.
AKI DOI
FINISHED~!!
It was down to the wire again, but we managed to get the manuscript in without any problems... Whew! ^o^
That's right!
I still have Aki Doi !!
THE ONLY THING I'M SURE OF
IS THAT I DON'T LOVE NATSUKI KOMIYAMA ANYMORE.
...
...
YUKIYO!!
Let's go to the morning market with your mom!
The mar-ket!
WAAAAGH
Sor-ry, sor-ry!
AHHAHAHAHAHAHA!
Oh my, they get along so well!

FARM FRESH FARMER'S MARKET

Wow, look!
They're selling shark! That's amazing!!
¥400
And just 400 yen!!

I'm out shopping with my mom and Natsuki ...

This is so surreal ...

What? You've never had shark before?

No! Does it taste good? Ah ha ha ha ha!

Not to mention that Natsuki is wearing my clothes.

I wonder if Mom always wanted me to get married and do this kind of thing with my wife ...

Yuki-yooo!

Isn't this place so much fun?!

Uh, is it?
You haven't been here since grade school, right?
You used to love coming here, but now...
Really? What a waste! You came all the way here from Tokyo, why not go out more?
You don't have enough hometown love!!

What...? It's not like I hate the place.
I just think I should be looking for work in Tokyo instead.
And I want to go back as soon as I'm better!

Huh...
I think you ought to stay here.
Why are you hung up on Tokyo?

Uhm...
Aki Doi's there, too...
Concerts... and friends...
Don't you have friends here, too? And you can just take a trip whenever there's a show you want to see.

You want Yukiyo to stay, too, don't you, Mom?
Hm?
Well, yes.
HEY.

I'd like to try living in a place like this, too...
HEY!

...
...
...
Please, don't get my mom's hopes up!
NO!!
Are you hungry, Na-tsuki?
There's a place where you can eat fresh-fried fish cakes!
OOOOOH!
I've heard about these before! I've always wanted to try some!!

OH.

WE DRANK.
IT WAS THE FIRST TIME
KLINK
Cheers! ☆
complete recovery, Pork Broth! ☆
"YEAH, IT DOESN'T TASTE QUITE RIGHT. IT'S BETTER BACK HOME."
"WHAT, REALLY? I HAVEN'T SPENT MUCH TIME IN THE COUNTRY-SIDE..."

"SERIOUSLY? THEN COME VISIT MY HOMETOWN!! YOU CAN STAY AT MY PLACE."
"HUH... I'D LIKE TO TRY GOING SOME TIME."
"THERE'S A BUNCH OF SPOTS I WANT TO TAKE YOU! WE CAN BUY FISH AT THE MORNING MARKET THAT MY MOM WILL COOK. IT'S SUPER TASTY!!"
"YOU'VE GOTTA COME! PROMISE ME!"

These, right?
OOH...
Let's try one.
Hot!
Ah!
!!
It's good.
Just like you said, Yukiyo.
OH.
Yeah...
THIS IS WHAT I WANTED TO DO FOR NATSUKI BACK THEN.
ALL OF THIS.
HA HA HA HA HA HA
SO YOU REMEMBERED YOUR PROMISE,
NATSUKI?
?
Are you watching this, Fatty Fuji?!
Your dreams came true!!

OH.
NOW I GET IT.
I'D ALWAYS BEEN LOOKING AT NATSUKI
THROUGH THE LENS OF MY PAST SELF.
Oh, I know. Can you send me a photo of myself?
Use your cell, I forgot mine!
Oh, sure ...
SFF
I FELT SO SORRY FOR MY PAST SELF THAT I COULDN'T FORGIVE HER IN THE PRESENT.

No, I can't just accept things like this!
I can't! I can't do it!
It's un-natu-ral!
I'm leaving!
STOMP STOMP STOMP STOMP
スタ スタ スタ スタ…
Hey…! Show me the pic!
A LOT HAS HAPPENED,
BUT I'M LIVING IN A FUTURE THAT I USED TO YEARN FOR.
BUT…
THE THINGS I COULDN'T DO THEN
I CAN DO
NOW.

They're attacking you, Yuma!

They're like old bearded guys or something~!

Take a picture, Nao~! ♡

Rinetics

It's so hot out...

KPOP

Maybe I should send the picture to Fujimoto, too...

Oh, but he might get mad that I didn't invite him...

AAH~!♡

CHUUTE~!

It's like I'm feeding a bunch of bearded men~!

Hey, Yukiyo, take a picture!

What are you doing?

Look! I'm being attacked by capy-baras!!

You're such an idiot. Ha ha!

I just took a video, see?

What, really? Lemme see!

Hey, Nao! Take a picture!

?
キョロキョロ
GLANCE GLANCE
DASH
ダッ

Huh ...? Uncle Yukiyo ?
Yeah ...
Wooow! He's on a date, isn't he?!

Aaah...
Yep,
yep,
yep,
yep,
yep,
yep,
yep.
NOD
NOD
NOD

I don't know the details,
but I guess after getting involved with all those women, Fujimoto has managed to make it this far.
Ah... That same gloomy boy who was always drawing manga in middle school...
She's so pretty...

SNIFF
SNIFF

Nao,
are you not gonna say hi?

chapter 29 ♥ END

M o t e k i   M i t s u r o u   K u b o

M o t e k i

M i t s u r o u K u b o

chapter 30 ♥ Stay Gold

4TH KODANSHA MANGA AWARDS

And the winner of the Shonen Manga division ...

is the author of *Magical Card Boy Justice!!*, Asuka Amaebi-sensei!

KLAP

KLAP

KLAP

KLAP

Please don't look so obviously disap-pointed!

She didn't have a hit for ten years after she debuted,
but once this series took off, Amaebi-sensei has kept it running for over 40 volumes!
STAB
And it seems it's had a smooth run the whole time. She's never once taken a break or missed a deadline.
STAB

Both you and Amaebi-sensei have made wonderful contributions to the magazine!!
There are people who recognize what you've done. Cheer up!
ZHAAAA
Oh! There you are, Omu-sensei!
Ah, editor-in-chief!!
I heard the news, it's too bad the live-action talks fell through.
...
Ah ...
AAA
Yes ...
ZHA
We are in a recession, though. What can you do?
And I mean, a high school girl as a head hostess ...?
Well,
I hope you can draw something that sells better for your next work!!
A decision was made to end his series.
You've only got two months left, Omu-sensei, please do your best!!

SLUUMP
...
...
Sen-
sei
...!
Would you like me to bring you some roast beef?
Oh, no.
He's been non-stop depressed for a while now...

How can I cheer him up...?

Uhm... Excuse me?
Are you Omu Ono-saka-sensei ...?
Eh?
FID
GET

AAH!
Uhm, I'm a fan!
I-I'm a big fan, too!
Would it be okay... to get an auto-graph?

AAH
whew...

GLANCE

That must be her, the manager that Akky was modeled after ...
WHISPER
Aaa aaaa aagh ...
And which editor was that?!
WHISPER
WHISPER
What, you think so?
She really is pretty ...
I wonder if they're dating ...
Oh, they have to be. My editor said it was true, too...
WHISPER

STARE
I'll go get you some-thing to drink, Sensei.
Oh. Okay.

Aah ...
There aren't even any manga authors I know here. This is so boring.
CHATTER
CHATTER
I wonder if Omu-sensei would be okay without me.
CHATTER
AH HA HA
REALLY?
I wanna go home ...

OH.

THAT'S WHAT I CAN TEXT FUJIMOTO ABOUT.

I guess ...
I'll email him today about being at a manga award ceremony ...
Let's see... "I feel lonely because I don't know anyone here... It'd be so nice if we could enjoy this together" ...
There we go ...
... ...

No!
What am I doing?! This sounds like totally forced sadness!
Then again, I haven't sent him many messages recently about how much I miss him, so maybe timing-wise it's OK...?
But he could read an email about me being at a party and take it as me boasting about how great and exciting Tokyo is, so no! I'm changing it!! I need to be more considerate of the fact that he's back in the countryside because of his health. No, no, no, gotta revise this! Something about how my life in Tokyo isn't super tough, though maybe it is a little tough...

Uhm ... Excuse me?

Yes?!
What is it?
SNAP
Oh.
Were you occupied with something just now? I'm sorry.

Yikes... What did I look like just now?
にこっ
GRIN
It's okay.

You're Omu Onosaka-sensei's manager, aren't you?
I saw you together just a moment ago...
Oh.
I'm an editor at the same magazine as the female authors who just got his autograph. My name is Yui.
DAISUKE YUI

Was it you? Are you the one spreading the rumor that Omu-sensei and I are dating?

Huh?

Are you not? Mr. Suzuki, Onosaka-sensei's editor, told me...

BAM

TSK

So it was Suzuki...

That's just his assumption. There's nothing between us!!

It's a problem when people think that!

I'm sorry.

I'll be sure to correct anyone who I might have told otherwise.

I'm glad it wasn't true.

I'd always wanted to ask you.

Ever since I talked to Mr. Suzuki,

I was hoping we could meet.

Oh.

You mean Omu-sensei?

He's still over there. Shall I introduce you?

... oh, yes.

HONESTLY,

I HAVEN'T BEEN ABLE TO FIGURE OUT WHAT TO WRITE TO FUJIMOTO LATELY.

WHEN I THINK OF FUJIMOTO, I SEE SOMEONE WHO'S STILL VULNERABLE, DISPIRITED, AND WAITING FOR SOMETHING.
AND THE LONGER WE'RE APART, THE MORE THAT IMAGE SOLIDIFIES ITSELF IN MY MIND.

I think it'd be easier if we saw each other again.
But he did say he couldn't go to this year's Fuji Rock with me...
I'll be going with friends again, but... I feel kind of guilty.

WHEN WE DON'T SEE EACH OTHER,

IT FEELS LIKE SOMETHING OTHER THAN LOVE IS GROWING INSIDE OF ME, AND THAT SCARES ME!!

I WONDER WHAT I COULD POSSIBLY BE DOING FOR HIM

WHILE WE'RE SO FAR APART...

I haven't gotten any pics from her since she sent me this one last month ...
I kinda feel like ...
I wanna ask her for a sexy one, but... I wonder if she'd get mad...

We haven't been able to meet up, but... it's kinda reassuring.
If it wasn't for Aki Doi, I'd be despairing at how little there is for me to dream about living here in the boonies...
I just wanna see her again and fool around ...!
INCOMING CALL
VVT VVT VVT VVT VVT
VVT VVT VVT
Ooh! ♡ Now that's mutual love!

It's me.
Fuji
?

Oh. It's you, Shimada
...
What's your deal? You've been neglecting me ever since you ran away
...
ROLL
I can tell you're not serious when you apologize twice.
Sorry, sorry.

So, what happened with you and Natsuki after I left?
You haven't said anything to me, either, so...

...
About that.

She's still in my home.
Wha ?!
It's been four days already
!

She's totally made herself at home... My parents have convinced themselves she's my girl-friend, too...
It's hard to kick her out on the street, you know... So I'm waiting for her to go on her own... y'know...?
...

Don't tell me you fell in love with Natsuki again.
SHAKE
No, I haven't! This is like, something done in memory of my past self!!
SHAKE

Y' know, I'm glad I got to finally come clean to you about everything.

I know I did something terrible, but you opened my eyes when you told me to live with pride.

I'm gonna talk to Yurie again.

I want to face what I did and take responsibility for it.

Well, my family found out, too, so I'm heading back to Tokyo.
Yui-chi!
STOMP
We're leaving now! There's not much time 'til the plane leaves!
Why wouldn't you tell us about this, you idiot?!
This problem is bigger than just you two now that you're married!!
STOMP
STOMP
STOMP
I know your grandpa may have been married four times and still had mistresses, but don't inherit that from him!!
...
...
I know! I'm almost ready!

Well ...
Uhm, that's all I wanted to say.
stay gold
Hi-STANDARD
MENU
Fuji.
See ya soon.
Yuki-yo.
Going some-where?
Yeah, just for a walk.
Hm?
GLANCE
SLURP

I CAN'T KEEP GOING LIKE THIS.
Oh!
Hello! Nice weather today!
I see you two are still getting along great! Eh heh heh! ♡

...Hey, Na-tsuki?
You said you quit your job. Why'd you do that?
Hmmm?
I just felt like it was about time to.

Who cares about that, anyway?
I feel so lonely, especially now that my sister got married...
Maybe I should get married, too.

Huh...?

Do you mean...

I'd like to try living over-seas...

Maybe take it easy on some tropical island.

What do you think? Would you wanna go too, Yukiyo?

What're you making that face for?
Ah ha ha ha...

Hey, let's try going this way.
Oh, this is my high school.
Huh! Is it summer break already?
WHEN I'M WITH NATSUKI, SHE SAYS THINGS THAT I NEVER EXPECTED TO HEAR.
Let's go inside, then!!
WHAAA?!

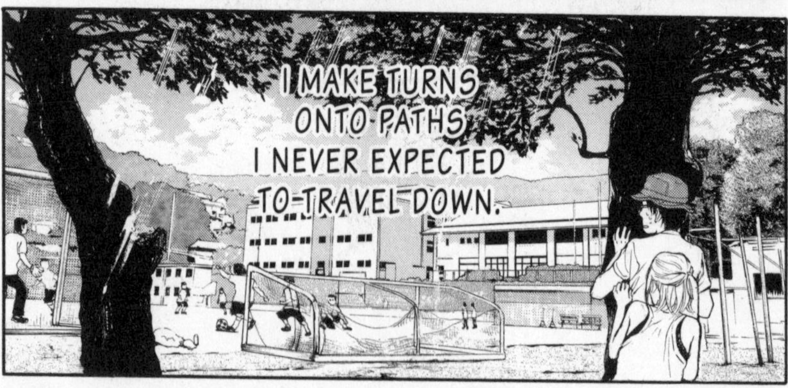
I MAKE TURNS ONTO PATHS I NEVER EXPECTED TO TRAVEL DOWN.

NO SHOES

MY LIFE TRANSFORMS FROM ONE WHERE I EXPECT NOTHING DRAMATIC TO EVER HAPPEN INTO SOMETHING ELSE ENTIRELY.

See some-thing, Yukiyo ?
No ...
The room is being used for something else.
It's not the way it used to be.

I remember that something happened here,

but I can't recall how I felt when I stood in this place.

Huh.

Do you ever wish you could go back to your high school days?

Huh? Never...

Ha ha. Me neither.

Even if I could,

I wouldn't want to just go to school every day and do my homework.

I WON'T FORGEEET

RAAAAAH!

STAY GOOOLD

But it's not like I could ever become popular playing in a Hi-STANDARD cover band at the school festival, either!!

I was just a loser who never even had a girlfriend,

but now that I'm standing here like this,

it makes me think that I've done pretty well for myself.

That is true.
The past doesn't mean anything in the present.
You're too hard-headed when it comes to your ideals, Yukiyo.
Don't you feel like you overthink them?

Huh ...?
I guess so...? I do overthink things...
I always have ...
GRIP
That's why you rejected me back then, right?
I'd already made up my mind about who you were.
There were so many things about you that I couldn't accept.
Even after you rejected me, I couldn't get over you.
I wasn't able to control myself at all.

But I'm better now!
Whatever the real you is thinking about, Natsuki, I want to face it!
BADUM
?!
Can we not talk about that kinda thing?
Give it a rest.

Huh ...?
What do you mean by that ...?
I'm just saying I want us to be completely open with each other. What's wrong with that?
So you want to ask me all kinds of things about myself,
then decide that I'm actually a lone-some person,
or that there's some-thing I lack ...
Men just love analyzing women on their own and pigeon-holing them into categories, don't they?
I hate the assumption or presumption that you understand the "real me."
There isn't even a "real me" I want you to understand.

Hey— What does that mean?
You don't like when someone gets the wrong impression of you, right?
If you looked inside the heads of a hundred people, you'd find a hundred different versions of me.
I can't be responsible for all of that.
I just don't care.

I don't like thinking too hard about stuff, anyway.

I tell random lies just because it seems like the thing to do in that moment.
I don't decide on ideals for myself.
I don't decide on a single person I'm in love with.
I'll even sleep with people I don't love.

I like living a life that doesn't go in the direction I think it's headed.
...
C'mon, Yukiyo...! Don't make that face.
GIGGLE

I FINALLY GET IT NOW.

In that case,

why don't we take a look inside?

YOU

SAW ME

AS A PATH YOU WEREN'T PLANNING TO TAKE.

You gotta be confident in yourself! C'mon, it'll be fine!!
You can be whoever you want to be.
You ...
You're just saying that... because you don't care what happens to me!
WHAAT?
YOU JUST HAPPENED TO TAKE THAT TURN. THAT'S ALL.
I DON'T EXIST INSIDE OF NATSUKI'S HEART.
I ONLY EXIST TO HER WHEN I'M IN FRONT OF HER EYES.
Like I just said ...
I don't care about the real Yukiyo.
THAT'S RIGHT.

I WOULDN'T BE ABLE TO CHANGE IF I STAYED IN THIS ROMANCE.
NOT EVER.

Heh heh ...
Yuki-yo?
Huh?
Are you laughing?

chapter 30 ♥ END

Final Chapter ♥ A Life Spent on the Edge

BWA HA HA HA HA HA
SERIOUSLY?
C'MON, LET'S GET GOING!
THUD
THUD
THUD
NO SHOES

... Yuki-yo.
Hey, some-one's com-ing.

Okay.

Yuki-yo?
...

Then let me stay like this until they're here.

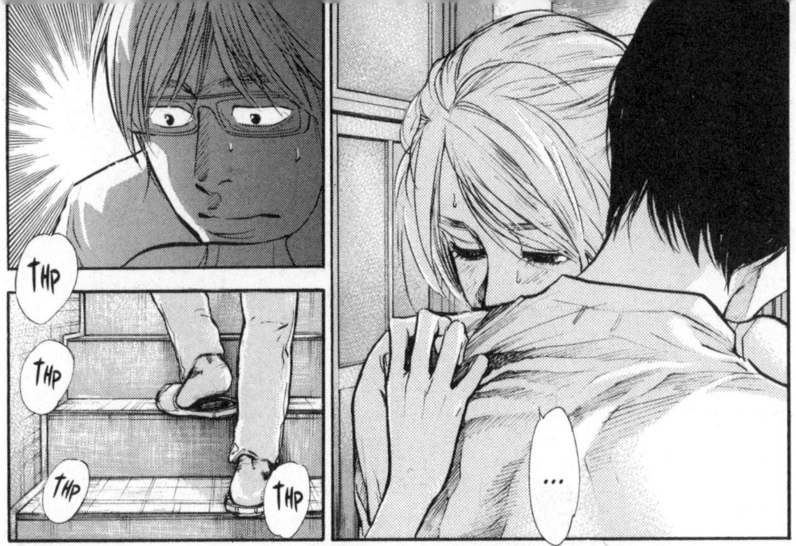
...
THP
THP
THP
THP

Hey!
Is someone there?

HEEEY

He's here.
Now what?

Oh...
Yeah.
I DON'T WANT IT TO END LIKE THIS.

Hello?
PEEK
ひょいっ

Hm?
I heard a voice...
DRAMA CLUB
THP
THP
THP
THP
THP
THP
Teacher!

DING
I KNOW I'VE NEVER BELIEVED IN A GOD ANY MORE POWERFUL THAN THE SHUFFLE FEATURE ON MY IPOD, BUT NOW I JUST HAVE THIS ONE REQUEST.
KLONG
KLANG
PLEASE DON'T LET
ANYONE INTERRUPT US.
I WANT TO REMEMBER THIS FOR AS LONG AS I CAN.
KLONG
EVEN IF IT'S ONLY BY ANOTHER SECOND.
BECAUSE I DOUBT I'LL EVER BE ABLE TO DO SOMETHING LIKE THIS AGAIN
UNLESS I PRAY TO GOD.

Yuki-yo?

I DOUBT I'LL EVER SEE HER AGAIN IF I LET GO NOW.

I thought I'd try to memorize what your nails look like.

Hmm.

Show me your teeth, too.

Heh. C'mon...

I think it might be time for me to head back... I've stayed here for a while, after all.

SEE?

You have a girl-friend, don't you?
...Yeah.
She's in Tokyo ...
Huh...
I figur-ed.

Maybe that's why you changed. Because you have a woman in your life now.
You're not like you were.

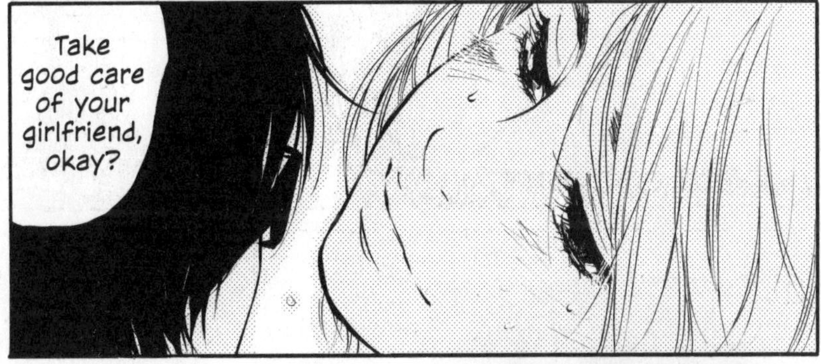
Take good care of your girlfriend, okay?

...
Yeah.
You know I will.

Aah...
It's hot in here ...

Why don't we leave ?

Hey, Yuki-yo?
...
You know, I think I'm good here.

Say thanks to your parents for me.
You can just send my stuff to my sister's place.

...
Could you let go of my hand, Fuji-moto?

NATSUKI!
There's still a lot more I need to tell you...!
BAMM

Huh?
What? I hope you're not snapping at me.
No, I'm not mad!
Not at all!
Though I do have some complicated feelings!!
GRASP

Uhm. So, I...
I wanted to ask you if you really think you can survive for the rest of your life on that cute, carefree, lovable side of you, and... uhh...
Uhh...
Are you planning on acting that way until you're old and gray?!
Your looks are only gonna go downhill from here. Or you'll become a cougar!
Or one day some guy is gonna stab you, and you're gonna be treated like a homewrecker, and the wife he cheated on is gonna fleece you for "emotional damages"...!
Whaa?

I don't want you going off and dying somewhere!

You need to find a place you can call home, somewhere you can really take care of yourself...

THE ONLY WORDS I CAN FIND...

Uhm...

ARE CLICHÉS.

You need to enjoy your life.

That's the side of you I love.

LIAR.

I STILL CAN'T FULLY LET GO.

BUT RIGHT NOW

I CAN'T BRING MYSELF TO SAY ANYTHING MORE TO HER.

... ...

TURN

Yuki-yo!

You know, I always wanted to tell you... I—

VROOOOOOOOMMM
HUH?!
WHAT?
I CAN'T HEAR YOU!
OOMM
WHAT DID YOU SAY?
NATSUKI!
HOOONK
OOOMM...

I REALLY MIGHT BE

SOME KIND OF GENIUS.

I'M NEVER ABLE TO SAY THE WORDS THAT REALLY MATTER.

I MISS THE WORDS THAT I WANT TO HEAR.

I CAN'T EVEN FIND A SONG THAT MATCHES HOW I FEEL RIGHT NOW.
No ...
This isn't it, either ...
Not this... Not this...
BIP
BIP

IT'D BE NICE IF I COULD WRITE SONGS AT TIMES LIKE THIS, BUT...
I've never written one before ...
and I think I'd only be able to come up with clichéd lyrics.
BAM

Hm?

PKAK
Don't tell me ...

Hello, Fuji-moto?
Is now a good time?
AKI DOI.
YES!
VZZZH ... ...
ZSHH ... ... I've... been thinking for a while.
Yeah? Uh-huh?
I can hear music in the back-ground... Is she at a show?
I think we should break up.

SHE FOUND OUT?!
No, that's impossible...
...Huh?!
Aah... B-Break up?!
Yeah.
I don't think it's good for us to always be so careful and concerned about each other.
It's not that I don't like you now, and I haven't found someone else I love, either.
Ah... Aki?
STOP!!
Hold... Hold on a second.
But when we're apart like this... it hurts me to know that I can't do anything for you.
But...
I'm sorry. I know I'm being selfish.
PRING
PRING
WATCH IT!!
SKREECH
WHOA!
KLATTER KLATTER
WAAGH!
VWOOOM
ブオー
SKREEK
BWAAAGH!!

WHAT IS THIS?
WHY DOES IT FEEL LIKE I KNEW THIS WAS COMING? LIKE I'VE BEEN HERE BEFORE...!
IS THIS...
MY PUNISHMENT FOR RUNNING AROUND AND ACTING LIKE I WAS HAVING MY MOTEKI?
...No, I'm not taking this sitting down!!
I should be furious that my call got cut off there!!
Aki Doi wasn't even done talking yet!!
Mom! Where's the closest Docomo shop??
THMP
THMP
Mom?!
Hm?
Mom?
Uuurgh...
?

MOM?!

DON'T DIE, MOM!

HOSPITAL

I'm okay. I just fell down the stairs and hit my head.

No, it's not okay. You look pretty banged up.

You even got a CT scan...

Natsuki is going to be so worried. Where'd she go off to right now?

I hadn't started getting dinner ready yet, is there anything you wanted to eat?

Uhm...

Well...

Natsuki has...

IT'S PROBABLY MY FAULT THAT THIS HAPPENED.

She went home.
She says thank you.
Already suspected it
Oh ...
SLUMP
Ah! Uhm ...!
You know, I'm gonna find a job here after all!
Today's my last day living as a bum! I promise !!

I've realized that I've been dreaming too big, after all.
I'm 30 now. There are a lot of things I should give up on so I can live a nice, modest life!
I'm only going to be a drag on you two if I keep living this way.
I'll do my best so that I can take care of you when you two are in your old age!

No, it's fine.
I wouldn't expect that from you now.

Do what you want to do.
I know your dad is annoying about it, though.
It's your life.
The last thing I want to see is you living a life you hate.
If there's something you want to do, give it everything you have.
MY PARENTS TAUGHT ME
THE KINDNESS THAT IS NOT TYING OTHERS DOWN.
MAYBE THAT'S WHY...
ALL OF MY CONNECTIONS TO OTHER PEOPLE ARE SO WEAK THAT THEY COME UNDONE WITH A LITTLE SHAKE.

I think we should break up.
I MUST REALLY BE AWFUL TO MAKE AKI DOI SAY SOMETHING LIKE THAT TO ME.

If only I could see her right now ...
Was I putting some kind of pressure on her?
Or may-be...

Oh ...
What day is it ?!
What? Why ?
BAM

Oh ...
So that's where she is right now...

GRIP
?!

Let's hurry back, Mom !
Huh ?
What? Hey ...
Hey, Yuki-yo!!

WHAT DOES AKI DOI THINK ABOUT ME INSIDE OF HER HEART?
Where are you heading?!
AWAY!!
This is because you spoil Yukiyo too much!
You always have!
He takes after his father!
Ah... And he used to be such a well-behaved boy...
I DON'T GIVE A DAMN!!
FUJI ROCK FESTIVAL'?
......

OH MAN, OH MAN, OH MAN, OH MAN...
OH MAN, OH MAN, OH MAN, OH MAN, OH MAN...

Wait, I'm here to find Aki Doi...
Crap...!
AH
YA
AY

EVEN IF I WASN'T WITH AKI DOI AT FUJI ROCK TWO YEARS AGO,
I HAVE A FEELING THAT I STILL WOULD'VE ENJOYED IT ON MY OWN.

MAYBE IT WOULD'VE BEEN BETTER IF I'D NEVER KNOWN THE FEELING

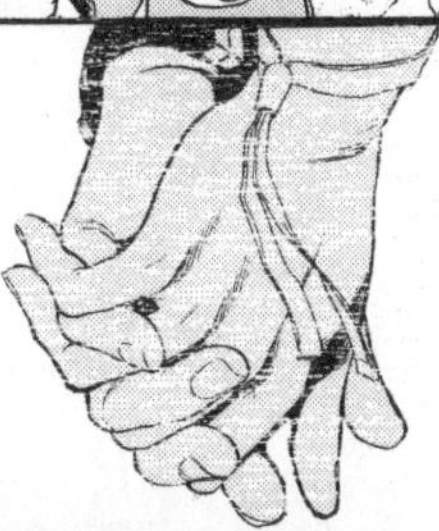

OF HOLDING HANDS WITH SOMEONE IN A LITTLE CORNER OF THE WORLD.

I OVER-LOOKED ALL SORTS OF WONDERFUL THINGS
WHILE I WAS STUCK IN A HAZE OF DESPAIR ABOUT THE WORLD AT LARGE...

SLUMP
I guess it really was hope-less ...

Miss Doi!
Your beer.
Oh! Thanks.
BAM
Who?
A guy...?!
THIS IS REALITY.
EVEN I WAS DOING ALL THAT STUFF WITH NATSUKI.
SHE'S NOT GOING TO JUST WAIT FOR ME. LIFE ISN'T THAT CONVENIENT.
AKI WOULD BE ABLE TO DATE WAY BETTER GUYS, ANYWAY.

SHE DIDN'T EVEN LOVE ME
TO BEGIN WITH.

You moron!!
Are you gonna run away with-out doing anything yet again?!
How unfaithful of a woman do you take Aki Doi for, you dumb-ass?!
Oh...
Show her who you are now!!
You suck, Fuji!
So you're still gonna run away? You haven't changed one bit.
THEY ARE REALLY THERE
I hate the assumption or presumption that you under-stand the "real me."
IN MY HEART.
I MET THEM ALL,
MADE THEM WORRY,
HEARD THEIR ENCOUR-AGEMENT,
AND NOW THE VOICES IN MY HEART HAVE MULTIPLIED.

AND I EXIST INSIDE OF ALL OF THEM, TOO, AS VERSIONS OF MYSELF THAT ARE DIFFERENT FROM THE REAL ME.
がばあっ
JUMMPP
AKI!!
AAAAAAH
アー

I'D ALWAYS THOUGHT THAT I DIDN'T DESERVE TO BE LOVED.
BUT REGARDLESS OF WHO I REALLY AM, THE ME THAT'S IN SOMEONE'S HEART IS ALWAYS GOING TO BE CHANGING, FOR BETTER OR WORSE.
I WAS NEVER ABLE TO FIGURE OUT IF I WAS ACTUALLY HAVING MY *MOTEKI* OR NOT,
THIS IS WHO I AM RIGHT NOW.
RA
BUT I THINK THAT "I" MUST HAVE BEEN MOVING AROUND ON MY OWN INSIDE OF THEM ALL.
I DON'T CARE IF IT DOESN'T ALL GET THROUGH TO HER.
I'M STILL GOING TO TRY TO TELL HER.

There was so much I wanted to say to you, Fujimoto,
but it's like I forgot it all the moment I saw your face.

THAT'S THE MOMENT

THAT THE ME INSIDE OF YOU BEGINS TO CHANGE.

Moteki ♥ END

M o t e k i

M i t s u r o u   K u b o

Motekis You Wouldn't Want to Read ⑦

Tokyo, 30 years later

WILL SOON BE OVER...

MY PARENTS HAVE DIED, I HAVE NO RELATIVES OR FRIENDS THAT I CAN RELY ON, AND I'VE LIVED ALONE IN TOKYO THIS WHOLE TIME.

I DRIFTED FROM ONE TEMP JOB TO ANOTHER, NOT LASTING LONG AT ANY ONE THANKS TO MY DEPRESSION. I HAVE NO SAVINGS, AND MY PROSPECTS ARE QUITE DIM.

If I could go back to that time...
Back to my *moteki*...
I'm sorry, I'm sorry, I'm sorry!!
I'm sorry for thinking of nothing but romance!
I will get a job! I'll get health insurance and start a retirement fund!

Motekis You Wouldn't Want to Read ⑧

Aki Doi ...
I ...
I love you more than anyone else in the world! Will you marry me?!

AAAA!
WHHOAA

You dummy ..!!

Saying that in front of everyone ...

OOOOOOH!

UNCLE

Fin

MOTEKI

Love Strikes!

Moteki
Mitsurou
Kubo

HELLO THERE, IT'S BEEN A WHILE.
THIS IS ITSUKA NAKASHIBA.
YUKIYO,
DO YOU STILL REMEMBER WHO I AM?
I...
HAVE NEVER FORGOTTEN WHAT YOU DID.
THAT DAY...
I COULDN'T HAVE BEEN ANY MORE CERTAIN.

Moteki: Girls' Side ♥ part 1

I DON'T HAVE
A CLUE WHAT
GUYS ARE
THINKING.

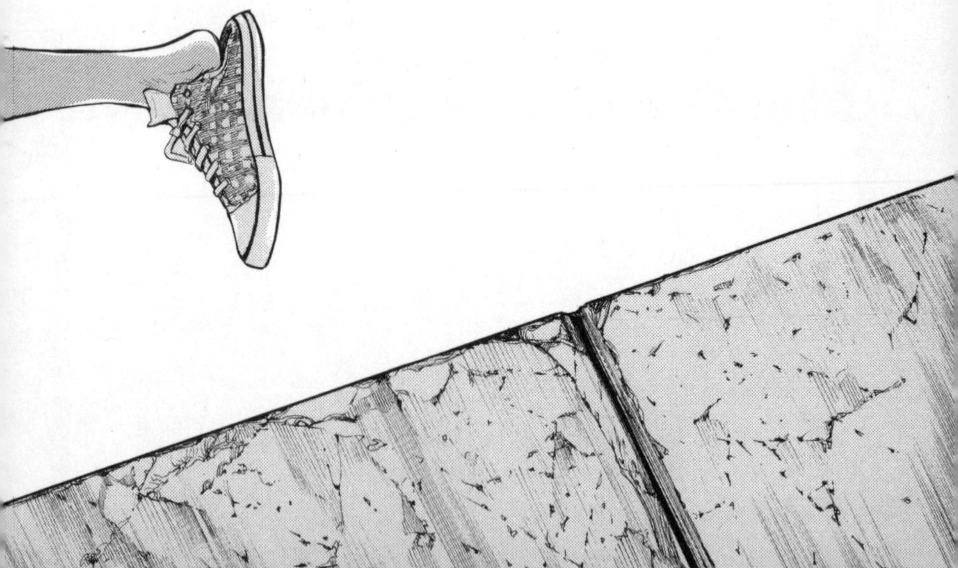

NO ONE KNOWS ABOUT THESE TEARSTAAAINS
THIS LOVE, THESE DREAMS THAT I LET GET AWAAAY
...MY PRIIDE ...!
SHAKA
SHAKA
You're like, really into this.
You can even sing Chage & Aska songs, Itsuka?!
Whew...
TNK...
Obviously something happened... God, I hope she's not like this all night...
I WENT TO KARAOKE WITH NAO AFTER-WARDS.
I-It's not every day I get an invitation from you, Itsuka!
I was thrilled, of course!
Why don't we invite some-one else while we're here?
Yurie was just saying on Twitter that she wanted to join.

Yurie?
Are you sure it's okay to get her out here this late? She's married, y'know.
She's always tweeting about how bored she is.
She said she's been lonely ever since she got married 'cause no one invites her out anymore.
It sounds like Shimada comes home late a lot, too.
Okay, I'm inviting her!
...
THEN YURIE MET UP WITH US.
NOW IT WAS THE THREE OF US.
Good evening!
No fair, you two were having fun all by yourselves...

That was fast. Your husband didn't mind?
What do you want to drink?
Oh, it's fine.
I need to have some fun every now and then, too!
Ooh, what should I sing! ♡

Oh.
It's nice to see you again, Itsuka.
Yeah! This might be the first time I've had drinks with you like this, Yurie.
Shimada was always with you every other time. This is exciting!
That's true... Heh heh...

DRIP
DRIP
DRIP
DRIP
What's wrong, Yurie?
Again?
THAT WAS WHEN I FIRST LEARNED
THAT SHIMADA WAS SLEEPING AROUND ALL OVER THE PLACE.
This time it was a girl working as a temp at his company...
I just found a note in his pocket...
Yikes... Isn't this right after the last girl?
Last time it was a sex worker who asked him out, right?
Sob... Sob...
What? Shimada pays for sex? Oh my God...
What a shock...
PLUS, IT SEEMED LIKE I WAS THE ONLY ONE WHO DIDN'T KNOW, AND THAT HIS CHEATING HAD BEEN GOING ON FOR AGES.
That was... close...
I'm glad I didn't do anything when every-one was around...
Wait, did Fuji know about this?

Wow. You must've had a rough time...
GLOOOOM
I had a pretty bad experience the other day, too...
Wha?!

So I tried to be really indirect about it and said, "I don't think I can do this anymore," and I don't mind if we break up but he borrowed money from me, but he hasn't returned it... but then I started feeling so sad that I...
That's awful! He's emotionally manipulating you, that's all!
WHEN DID ALL OF THIS HAPPEN TO YOU TWO...?
How did I miss all this?

I'm sorry for talking about all this heavy stuff, Itsuka...
You must be surprised to hear this...
Sorry...
Uh...
Actually... Me, too...

SORRY.
I TOLD THEM ALL ABOUT YOU AND ME (MINUS THE STUFF WITH SHIMADA).
But ... Like ...
the other woman really was beautiful... Like, I could never hope to be on her level...
I just don't think I'm enough to fill the hole Fuji's complexes have dug...
Fuji! That bastard! He makes such a fuss over still being a virgin, but he's so conceited! How could he be two-timing? No way!
He doesn't realize that you're being nice to him because you're his friend.
Shameless.
BAM BAM
Er ...
Well ...
Yeah ...
What are you, stupid?!
Why would you make us back you up on that?!
You gotta be more confident, Itsuka!
I think I spun it a little too much in my favor...
AND I'M ALSO SORRY THAT I MADE YOU SOUND LIKE A TOTAL BAD GUY.
No, but... Really, I'm not that beautiful...
STOP SAYING THAT KIND OF THING!! YOU CAN'T GIVE UP!!
I never knew I could be scolded this much for not being confident...

AND I'D JUST LEARNED A PAINFUL LESSON

THAT I NEED TO BE DOING MORE.

TREMBLE
TREMBLE
Uhm... You're still young, Itsuka. People will be interested in you as you are.
But I think you'd be cute wearing make-up, too.
Oh, that's it!
We'll do your make-up!
That's great!
They have costumes at this karaoke place, too. We can cosplay!
SNAP

Whaat?! No, no, that's too embarrassing!

Look up.

Decorative Eyelash

IT WAS THE FIRST TIME IN MY LIFE I'D EVER HAD MAKE-UP PROPERLY APPLIED.

So?
IT WAS
PRETTY HEAVY MAKE-UP.

Whoa ...
Whoa ...!

It's cute!
Yeah?
You should start wearing it more!

So this is all I can manage, even if I really try...
Awww...
I already knew that I don't have much to work with...
HEY!
WHY'S THIS GETTING YOU DOWN?!

I get it. I'm barely worth anything as a woman. You can stop now...
Thank you very much ...
Itsuka!
C'mon! Let's all sing a SPEED song together!

Oh god, that guy in the hallway is laughing ...
Who cares?! Don't worry about him!
NO. 1
We're having fun, that's all that matters!

YOU TWO...

EVEN THOUGH

YOU'RE HAVING A TOUGHER TIME THAN I AM...

EVEN IF I DON'T HAVE A BOYFRIEND,

I HAVE FRIENDS WHO'LL CHEER ME UP.

AND THANKS TO THEM, I DIDN'T END UP FEELING TOO DOWN ABOUT EVERYTHING.

DISPLAY YOUR ENTRY BADGE WHEN ENTERING THE PREMISES. IF YOU DO NOT HAVE AN ENTRY BADGE, SEE SECURITY AND FOLLOW THEIR INSTRUCTIONS.

AFTER ALL OF THAT, I DON'T WANT TO KEEP DRAGGING THIS BAGGAGE AROUND.

I HAD ALWAYS

WANTED TO CHANGE.

Hey, Naka-shiba. Naka-shiba !!

Where'd you go ?!

Yes ?

How long is this thing gonna sit here? It's in the way!

On it!

Hey! Next scene is...

CHATTER

Over here!

CHATTER

WHEW...

CHATTER

I went to the trouble of getting eyelash extensions,
but no one is saying a thing.
Maybe they aren't cute ...?

KPOP
Oh.
I got a text.

I set up a mixer with some salarymen!
Nao's coming, too!
Ooh!

It'll be my first mixer ...
And it's with salarymen...
GLOOOOM

But it's not like Fuji is the last man on Earth!
Now that I got these extensions, I should go out ...

NEW YEAR'S PARTIES
VARIOUS FOOD AND DRINK PLANS
GROUP FUN!
WE TAKE RESERVATIONS
Let me introduce you.
This is my friend, Nao.
Hello!
And this is Itsuka.
Nice to meet you!
Had them pick everything out

Uhm ...
A lot of people came today, huh?
More than I thought.
Well, it's also an end-of-year party ...
Now, eat up!!
Anyone else want a beer?
M... Me, too!
Yowza, you're so young!

Wasn't this supposed to be a two-on-two mixer, Yurie?
AH HA HA HA
That's what I was told, but... it sounds like it turned out this way 'cause their company is nerdy and their employees aren't able to meet many girls. I'm so sorry...

Oh, you're going to winter comiket?
That's amazing! I've never read any stuff for guys before...
CHIT
CHAT
Oh, but my big brother is a huge otaku! I used to rummage through his room all the time.
Wow, what a cool phone! Who made it?
ACK

Thanks for today! Let's go drinking again!
Okay!
Well, the three of us are off to chat on our own. Good-bye!
THANKS FOR COMIIING !!

KLOP
KLOP
Oh, I'm so sorry!
Let's pretend that never happened!
Huh?
KLOP
KLOP
They even went Dutch on the bill!!
That wasn't a mixer, they just had us join a company party!
It's always like that when I go drinking in groups...
And just like always, you had too much to drink!!

Those guys were no good at all.
They were kinda passive when they talked, too... They seemed like good people, but still.
We're all exhausted from trying to keep the conversation going. I wish they talked more!
And the age gap was too big...
All I can say...
is that they'll never get married at that rate.
I wish I could get yelled at by someone like you all day, Miss Yurie! ♥
Uh-huh!
Ended up being the most popular

In fact, they were barely acting like men at all.
How are we supposed to feel excited around guys like that?
It's like I'd never want to be more than friends with them.
Even being friends would be tough...
...

I USED TO NEVER ACT VERY FEMININE AT ALL.
WERE GUYS ALWAYS DISAPPOINTED IN ME THE WAY THESE TWO ARE DISAPPOINTED?

FUJI WAS PROB-ABLY THE SAME ...
...
... ka

Itsuka?
Yes ?

I'll set an-other mixer up.
I know you'll be able to find a nice boy-friend.

And me ?
Oh, sorry, sorry ...

Yeah.

IT'S NOT EVEN ABOUT ME WANTING A BOYFRIEND ANYMORE.
I'VE JUST STARTED TO ENJOY HAVING FRIENDS WHO WANT ME TO ACT MORE FEMININE.

I KNOW THAT I HAVE MY LIMITS, NO MATTER HOW HARD I TRY. I'LL NEVER BE ABLE TO BECOME SOME KIND OF PERFECT WOMAN.
BUT IN THAT CASE, I MIGHT AS WELL SAY SCREW IT AND ENJOY BEING A WOMAN.

I'M JUST BEING MY USUAL SELF, THE WAY I'VE ALWAYS BEEN AT WORK. I'M USED TO GUYS BECOMING MY DRINKING BUDDIES AND NOTHING MORE.
FORTUNATELY (?) NO ONE HAS REALLY TRIED TO MAKE ANY KIND OF MOVE ON ME.

I COULDN'T HANDLE GOING OUT AND PLAYING AROUND ALL THE TIME.
AH!
WORK IS AS BUSY AS EVER, SO I'M BACK TO CONSTANTLY TURNING DOWN INVITATIONS TO GO OUT.
I gotta get to work!

GETTING ESPECIALLY CLOSE TO MEN STILL FEELS EMBAR-RASSING,
SO I ALWAYS END UP TALKING TO OTHER GIRLS INSTEAD.
The iPhone is pretty good.
Really?
Again, Itsu-ka?!

NAO MET SOMEONE NICE, BUT SHE'S BEEN DEPRESSED EVER SINCE HE DUMPED HER.
Agh, this is so depressing...

Ugh... Again...
IT'S HARD TO INVITE YURIE OUT, NOW THAT SHIMADA'S CHEATING IS UPSETTING HER AND THEY'RE FIGHTING ALL THE TIME.

THEY BOTH WERE SO ENCOURAGING TOWARDS ME,

BUT I DON'T KNOW WHAT TO DO FOR THEM. WHAT CAN I SAY TO THEM AS SOMEONE WITH NO ROMANTIC EXPERIENCE?

A NEW SEASON IS STARTING.
HEY, NAKA-SHIBAA!
AWA STUDIO

Yes?
Sorry!
MY EYELASH EXTENSIONS HAVE COMPLETELY FALLEN OFF.

I guess I'm back to normal... Actually, I've been so tired lately that I feel like I'm getting even less feminine by the day...
My hair's really gotten long...

?!

Hello?
Nao?
Oh!
Can you talk right now, Itsuka?
Sure.

I just heard from Shimada.

Fuji herniated his back and is going to his folks' place.

WHAT?!

He's already getting ready to move and they're doing a farewell party the day after tomorrow at Shimada's place. Do you want to come?

It sounds like he's staying the night. It's fine if it's late after work, you should show up.

AH

Why now, when my face looks like this...?
... Sorry... I... still don't think I can...
Oh... Yeah, I get it.
I'll tell him you're busy with work, then.
NAO
Yeah. Thanks...
Say hi for me.
HEY, FUJI.
WHY DO I KEEP TRYING TO TALK TO YOU LIKE THIS EVER SINCE THAT DAY?
AM I...
NEVER GOING TO SEE YOU AGAIN?

Fuji's... still there.

BADUM
BADUM
Crap.
Suddenly showing up at his place would just make me seem like a super-annoy-ing girl!!

*IMAGINED
What would he think ...?
You decid-ed to come ?
I always wanted to apol-ogize ...
...NO, THAT'S NOT GONNA HAP-PEN.

Oh ...
Hold on, let me go out-side.
GCHAK
BADUM
Yeah, I'm okay. The re-ception is just bad inside ...
That's Fuji's voice!
WHPP
BADUM
BADUM
BADUM

Upsie.

HUP

Oww ...

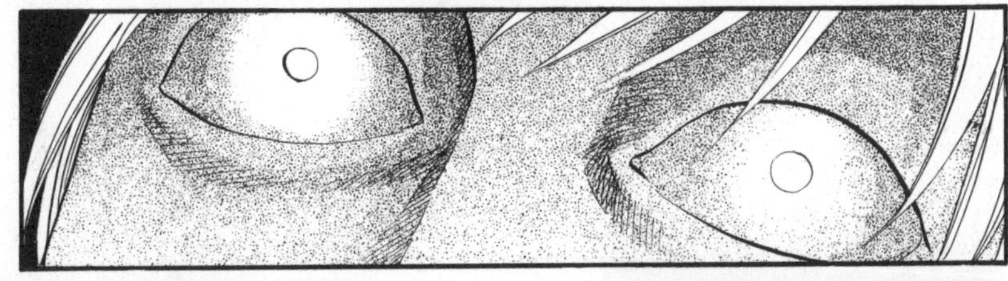

Hellooo? Can you hear me, Aki?

"Aki" ...?!

Yeah, I'm fine.

Yeah.

I think I'll manage the move tomorrow somehow.

FUJI... GOT FAT ?!

OH... IT'S HER...

IT WAS A SHOCK TO SEE HIM SO FAT...
BUT IT WAS AN EVEN BIGGER SHOCK TO HEAR THAT HE'S HAPPILY DATING THAT WOMAN.
SOMEWHERE INSIDE,
I WAS HOPING TO SEE A FUJI THAT WASN'T SO HAPPY.
I'M THE WORST.
I'M AS PATHETIC AS YOU CAN BE.
HAAH
HAAH
HAAH
HAAH
BADUM
Whose number is this ...?
I haven't given Fuji the number for this phone...
WHIP
... Yes ?

Hello, Itsuka? It's me.
Miyuki, we met at the mixer. Do you remember me?

Oh, hi. Nice to hear from you.
So, I'm actually drinking with some friends under some cherry blossoms. Do you want to come?
Ah ha ha ha
Remember how you said you wanted to do a flower viewing?

Ooh, nice ...
I'll head over now, then.

Oh ...
So the cherry trees are already in bloom ...

THANK GOODNESS.

I DON'T KNOW IF I COULD STAND BEING ALONE TONIGHT,
AND I DON'T FEEL LIKE I CAN TALK TO YURIE OR NAO YET, EITHER.
?!
Oh, there you are.
Heeey, Miyuki!

Oh, Itsuka?
Whoa, it's all guys!
I didn't recognize you. You look so different from the mixer.
Ah ha ha ha, this is the regular me. Sorry about that.
What's up! Nice to meet everyone!
WHUMP
WHO CARES ABOUT BEING FEMININE?
You really drink, Itsuka!
Whoa, that's great!
Let's keep 'em coming!
I'M DONE
THINKING ABOUT THINGS.
VVVT
VVVT
VVVVVT
YOU HAVE 1 NEW MESSAGE
You got mail.

Hm?

Huh ...?

Who was this again ...?

Oh ...

Now I remember.

Mr. Yoneda, that guy from sales who came to the mixer at the end of last year.

That's a salesman for you ...

Wait, didn't this guy say he was divorced? "Where are you now?" What?

VVVT

Ah!

A call?!

Whoa.

It's Mr. Shimizu from work.

Nakashiba!

Yeah, hello?

Hey, Nakashiba!! Pick up the damn phone when I call you! What the hell're you doing right now?!

Uhm ...

I'm at a friend's flower viewing party in the park ...

We're doing one too, so get over here right now!!

You okay? Are you drunk?

We're in Shinjuku.

VVVT

WHOA!

...

Yes?

Hello?

RISE
Oh ...
Yes!
Yoneda here, did you get my text?
We're having a flower viewing party in Shinjuku right now. Wanna come?
Everyone wants to see you again, Itsuka!
Huh ...?
BIP BIP ...
BIP BIP ...
Oh, sorry. I'm getting another call... I'll call you back.
Yes, hello ?
Hey, Itsuka! How've you been?
You've been pretty distant lately, huh ?
I'm drinking in Shinjuku right now. Wanna come out ?
Just the two of us. It's been a while!
Hel-looo ?
Hey, Itsuka! You're up!
We were just playing a drinking game, you should join!
Uhm ...
Here, draw a slip.
Huh ?
Huh ?!
Hold on, could this be ...

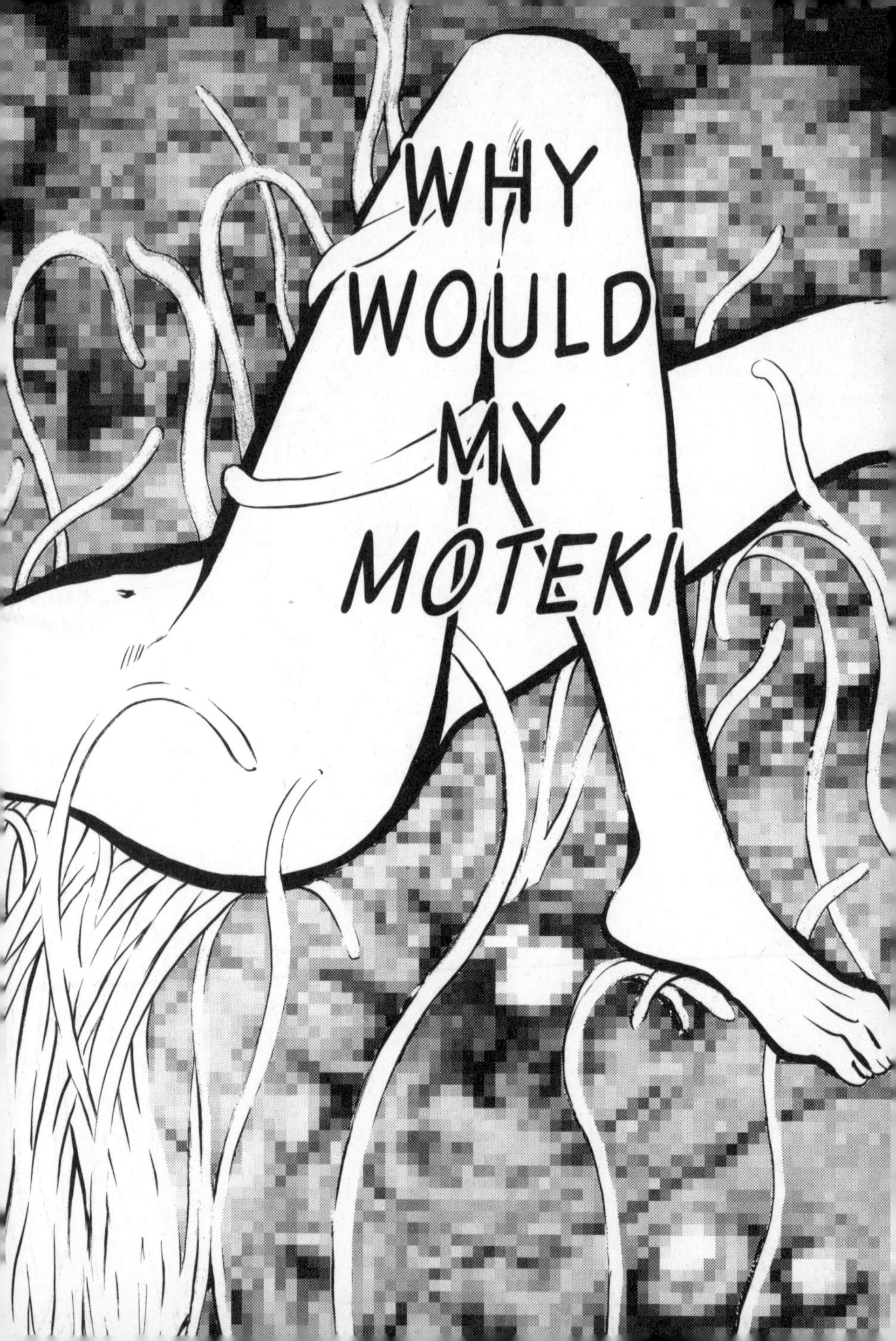
WHY
WOULD
MY
MOTEKI

COME RIGHT NOW?!

AAAGH
Sorry, sorry! I got the wrong picture in my head!
So, who's king?
MEEE!

?!
#1 has to kiss the King!
What? Me?
You saw my number, huh?
Yep, with me!

IS THIS REALLY HOW A *MOTEKI* IS SUPPOSED TO WORK?

part 1 ♥ END

I'M EXCEPTIONALLY UNFEMININE TODAY.
Ponytail to hide bed head
Tanned from a recent shoot
Slumped back
No makeup. In fact, face is greasy
chain store hoodie (men's)
¥1,980 bra
Socks bought at a convenience store (dirty)
Plain t-shirt
Nails split from cutting them too short
Multiple bruises on knees
I ATE A TON OF BARBECUE JUST YESTERDAY AND I THINK I SMELL LIKE GARLIC, AND I'VE BEEN PRETTY CONSTIPATED RECENTLY, AND I HAVE A PIMPLE, AND... WAIT, DID I WASH MY FACE THIS MORNING...?
*In such an unattractive state that even she realizes it

AND YET...
Who's king?!
Oh, it's me!
For real?!
WHAT'S GOING ON HERE...?

AND I'VE GOTTEN MYSELF INVOLVED IN A DRINKING GAME WITH GUYS I JUST MET.
Number 2 and 3!
Kiss for 10 seconds!
Aagh, they are really doing it!!

Moteki: Girls' Side ♥ part 2
ITSUKA NAKASHIBA

cut
these out and
have fun! ♡

BWA HA HA HA HA HA
YEAAAH!
SERIOUSLY, I CAN'T!
OKAY, WHO'S THE NEXT KING?!

Here!!
I'm King!
Oh, you're King again?

You know you haven't given any orders yet, Itsuka.
Let's hear some sexier orders!
No way!!
BOO BOO BOO
Uhm, in that case...

Number 4.
The dirtiest story in your life!
WHAA? THAT'S IT? DON'T RUN AWAY!
Oh, me?
I don't have anything...

Whew... I'm glad there's someone other than me who's not into this.
C'mon, tell us that one story. About how you and your girlfriend !#^#ed and X^*$ed on your college campus, and then you #&@!X&#ed like crazy after that, remember?
Oh, that story? That was just us being young...
But yeah, I guess we did #&^!...
Even a guy who looks that straight-laced...
ドン引き
CREEPED OUT

I MUST HAVE THE LEAST ROMANTIC EXPERIENCE OUT OF EVERYONE HERE.
Okay, next.
Who's King?
Me!
Okay, number 2 and number 6...
Kiss while you grab her breasts!
BAM
Oh.
Me?

Oooh!
It's finally Itsuka's turn!
No fair, Goto!
AAHH ♡
Ack...
I really got Itsu-ka?

Huh?
PAT
Uhm...
Well... Sorry about this.
Uh... Uhm...
Are we really going to do this?!

ARE WE REALLY GOING TO DO THIS?!
Wait ... I...

WHOA, THAT'S SUPER HOT!
OOH
AAH!
WHOAA
OH MY GOD!
HURRY UP AND GO TO THE NEXT ONE!

Oh, you're such an idiot.
Who cares about that. Just hurry up and kiss me. C'mon!
Mmmwah!
Seri-ously, Sumi?
You're so funny!

Fine, then let's brow-kiss!
RUB RUB
What's that?
You've never heard of it! We kiss with our eye-brows!
What? Isn't that even dirtier? Noo!
What do you mean, no?
c'mon!

I'm here for that drink.
Oh ...
Itsu-ka.

WHAP
OWW!

Oh, I gotta go!
Hey! Wait ...

BTAM
...

KRIK
Anyway. I was waiting for you, Itsuka. I thought you might not show up.
I see you're as lively as ever, Sumi.

Hm?
Why the long face?
Some-thing happen?

Yeah ... You see.

I didn't know who else to tell about this, so...

Hm? Yes? Go on?

GLOOOM

...

In other words,

a lot happened with Fuji and Shimada.

You were traumatized by the realization that guys like pretty women.

You left mixers empty-handed and are drowning in work.

And you discovered today that Fat Fuji has a girlfriend,

so you went to the park in desperation and made out with a bunch of guys during a drinking game.

...

Huh.

I see.

I used to do that all the time, too ...

I made girls do all kinds of naughty stuff to me whenever it was my turn as king.

So, Itsuka, you've now become a fine lady who's capable of showing off every orifice in public?

NO, I DIDN'T DO THAT!!

BAM

It was just with a couple of guys ...

And with Miyuki, too...

It felt like we were having fun, that's all. I went along with the flow and ignored my own feelings.

Everyone was drunk, though, and it got tedious so we stopped ...

So what's the pro-blem? It's not like you have a boy-friend right now.
Did no one there interest you?
I don't want to meet a guy like that!!
HMF

So you're not going to go to the party that the salary-man you met at the mixer is having?
He just invited you, didn't he...?
HUH ...?
It's not like we got along all that well ...
Then why not go to the one your coworkers are holding? Are there no guys at work you're interested in?
No way!
I can't think of them like that!
HMM...

Do you like Shi-mada?
He's mar-ried.
What about Fuji?
He has a girl-friend.
What about me?
...

C'mon, say some-thing!

SMAK

OWW!

Aargh... Geez...

I just don't know ...

If you don't know, you just need to find out.

Let's figure out who made your heart beat the fastest out of everyone you met today.

Huh?

SFF
SFF
Go to that flower viewing party with the guy from the mixer.
Then go to the one with your work buddies and be as girly as you can be.
What? No way, I can't do that!
Your *moteki* came today. Don't waste it.
Actually, I get the feeling I could do it with you today.
Come back here if no one makes your heart race.
Then we can go to some hot spring resort.
I know a good place to stay.
Don't worry. I don't hit it and quit it.
C'mon, say something! Ha ha!

IT DOESN'T MATTER WHAT MY HEART DOES...
IT'S NOT LIKE ANYONE IS GONNA SERIOUSLY BE INTERESTED IN ME, RIGHT?!

I think it was around here...

BUT...

Oh!

Naka-shiba! Over here!

Oh, hi... It's been a while.

Sorry for the sudden invite. Thanks for coming!

Oh, everyone's over there. C'mon this way!

Anyone else want a beer?

I DON'T REALLY REMEMBER HIM, BUT... I THINK THAT WAS THE SAME YONEDA FROM SALES I EXCHANGED EMAIL ADDRESSES WITH.

Yowza, you're so young!

I'm surprised you knew it was me.

I had a ton of make-up on last time...

Huh? No, I knew it was you right away!

That's a salesman for you...

HA HA HA...

I wonder if I'm gonna let everyone else down 'cause I don't have any make-up on, though...

Sorry for not contacting you since the mixer.
Oh, no.
All these single guys and they're still awful at inviting girls over.

It always has to be me ...

I forget, was he married ...?

What were the others like ...?
Sumi said to find the guy that made my heart beat the fastest, but...
I don't feel like I can make any of them interested in me right now, not like this...

It still gets cold at night, huh?
That is true ...
It's gotten so chilly.

...

Wanna go over there for a second?
Huh?
Uh, ahh...

TUG

Uhm.
Huh?
Hunh?! Is Yoneda drunk?
Wait, is this—

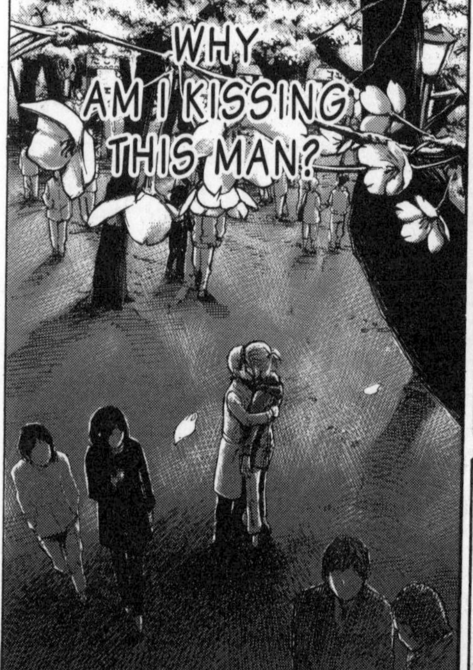
WHY AM I KISSING THIS MAN?

IF OUR GENDERS WERE REVERSED, IT'D PROBABLY MAKE FOR A DIRTY LITTLE STORY ABOUT GETTING SEDUCED BY SOME SULTRY HOUSEWIFE. SO WHY DOES THIS FEEL SO DEPRESSING?
I REMEMBER HEARING AN ACTOR SAY THAT SHE WAS IN SO MANY SEX SCENES THAT SHE DOESN'T FEEL ANYTHING DURING THEM NOW. I WONDER IF IT'S LIKE THAT.
I THOUGHT MORE FEMININE WOMEN GOT DRAGGED INTO SITUATIONS LIKE THIS. SO WHY ME?
I CAN ONLY ASSUME HE THINKS I'M AN EASY TARGET...
Why am I never the one taking the lead ...?
I can't believe how fast my brain is cooling off here...
Maybe I really am easy today... Hah!

Uh... Uhm... Isn't everyone else waiting for you ...?
Hm ?
It's fine.
They won't notice if I'm gone.
Why don't we go to a hotel?
Agh!

He's moving so fast!! Well, that's a salesman for you!
Wait, no —!
Uhm, I...
It's okay, it's okay ...
C'mon, touch me ...
I'm already so...
AAAGH!

Hey!
NAKA-SHI-BAAA!
THAT VOICE...!
BAM
Shi-mizu from work?!

He saw me!
BADUM BADUM
Oh!
This isn't what you think.

Na-kashi-ba.
Every-one already left.
You're late. The party's over and we're already onto the after-party.
You com-in'?

Oh, yeah!
Then hurry up. This way.

HALT

JOLT

Nakashiba.

Are you quitting your job?

Flat-faced girls like you always seem to quit in no time flat.
It's like you're easily frustrated or something.
Flat-faced?
You'd
better not be quitting.

I'm not going to quit!
I'm not chasing after a man, either!
All I have is my work!
okay, okay.
Sorry for thinking you were gonna do something dirty...
HONESTLY,
I FEEL RELIEVED.

I FEEL A LOT MORE COMFORTABLE WHEN PEOPLE WANT ME FOR THINGS THAT DON'T HAVE TO DO WITH MY BEING A WOMAN.

I HAD A LOT OF BROTHERS AT HOME. I ALWAYS PLAYED WITH THE BOYS AT SCHOOL, TOO. I GOT USED TO HANGING OUT WITH GUYS!

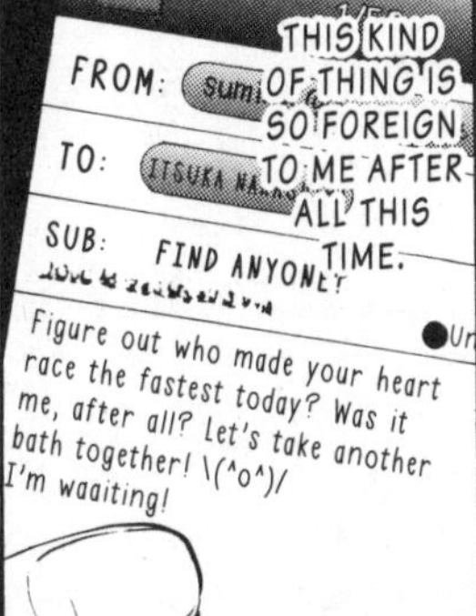
THIS KIND OF THING IS SO FOREIGN TO ME AFTER ALL THIS TIME.
FROM:
TO: ITSUKA
SUB: FIND ANYONE?
Figure out who made your heart race the fastest today? Was it me, after all? Let's take another bath together! \(^o^)/ I'm waaiting!

LET'S DECIDE WHO MAKES YOUR HEART BEAT THE FASTEST TODAY.

Y' know ...
I'm just going to ignore this one...

WHOA!

?!

ank 3G
iichi Shimada

Hello?

Hey, Itsu-ka.
I just got a call from Sumi.
He said there's some-thing you wanted to ask me?
WHAT DID HE JUST SAY ?!
Huh ?
Oh... I wanted to talk to you about, uh...

Hm ?!
Naka-shiba's talking to a guy!
Invite him !!
He's a friend! Just a friend!!

Eve-ning!

YEAAAAH

HE'S HERE !!

So you're Naka-shiba's man? Pretty hand-some guy.

Bet you get a lot of girls.

Oh, no ...

I'm a married man.

Another married man ...?!

He already rejected me once ...

Don't get the wrong idea!

OH. RIGHT.
HE REJECTED ME BEFORE.
I know I've never said a thing until now,
but I really like you, Shimada.
Yeah. I know.
Huh?
I knew and just pretended that I didn't notice.
Sorry.
It's been a while. How are you?
You've been out with Yurie, right?
Sounds fun, invite me some time!
Uh... Sure...
This time it was a girl working as a temp at his company...
Yikes... Isn't this right after the last girl?
I'VE HEARD ALL YOUR SECRETS !!

SHIMADA HAS SUCH A BEAUTIFUL WIFE,
AND YET HE'S CHEATING ON HER WITH ALL THOSE WOMEN.

He probably
couldn't see me as a woman,
NOW THAT I THINK ABOUT IT...
And it's not like I wanted to be a home-wrecker.
I couldn't take someone else's man!

I WAS SO IN LOVE WITH SHIMADA,
I'm hanging out with Fuji!
BUT I NEVER ONCE IMAGINED
THAT HE COULD BE IN LOVE WITH ME.

So? What did you want to talk about, Itsuka?

Oh...

WELL, A LOT HAPPENED TO ME TODAY.
?

Ah.
I won't be able to make it to Fuji's farewell party, but could you say hi to him for me?
I've got work ...
Huh? You're not coming ?
C' mon ...!
TO-DAY
I LEARNED THAT FUJI HAS A GIRLFRIEND.
AND I KISSED A LOT OF PEOPLE.
Hey, Naka-shibaa! Sing us some-thing on the karaoke ma-chine!
You never sing !
Hear that ?
Whaaat?
BUT...
I don't have any idea what I should sing!

CLOSE
Damn...
We drank 'til morning.
Ah, I had a lot of fun drinking with you guys tonight!
Ah ha ha ha! Let's do this again, Shimada!!
WHRRR

THUD
THUD
Whoa!

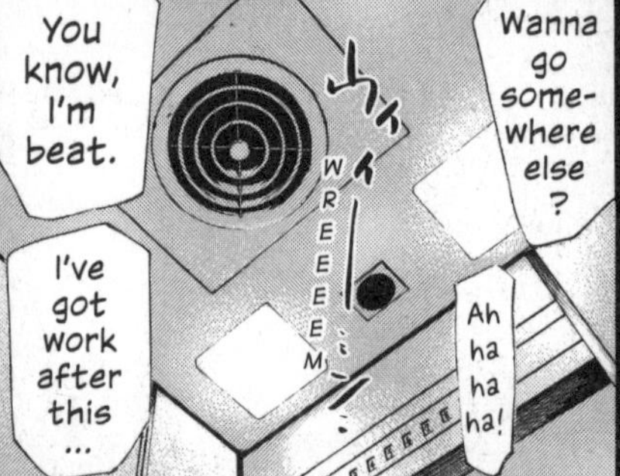
Wanna go somewhere else?
Ah ha ha ha!
You know, I'm beat.
I've got work after this...
WREEEEM

AH HA HA HA
YAWN
AND SO...

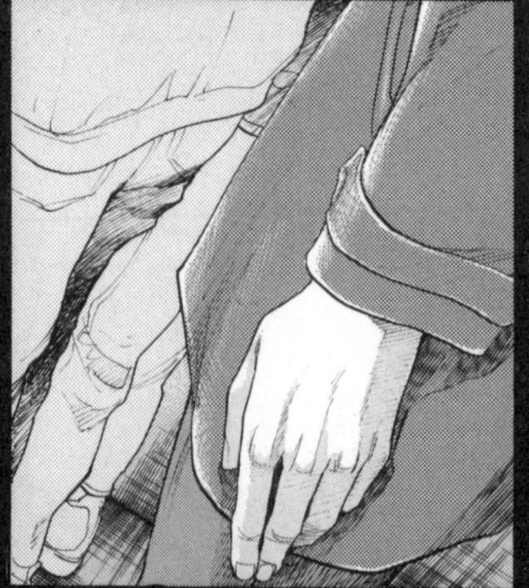

I WAS ABLE TO KISS PEOPLE I BARELY KNOW...
BADUM
BUT I CAN'T EVEN HOLD THE HAND OF SOMEONE I LOVED!
BADUM
BADUM
BADUM
BADUM
THIS IS MY LIMIT.

SQUEEZE
ぎゅっ

AMAZING.
AH HA HA HA HA
SERIOUSLY ?!
DING
WHRRR
THE WORLD IS AN INCREDIBLE PLACE.
Yikes ...
Look at how bright it is already.

BAM
Itsu-ka?
I WAS ABLE TO HOLD THE HAND OF THE MAN I LOVED THE MOST IN MY LIFE.
Sorry, I gotta go!

I'D NEVER BE ABLE TO DATE THE MAN WHO JUST HAPPENED TO BE MY FIRST, BUT HE STILL CHEERED ME ON.

I WAS ABLE TO KISS PEOPLE WHO DIDN'T EVEN LIKE ME THAT MUCH.

THERE ARE STILL A LOT OF THINGS IN THIS WORLD

THAT I DON'T UNDERSTAND.

HAA

HAA

I DON'T HAVE ANY NEW ANSWERS,

BUT IT'S SO FULL OF DREAMS.

BUT RIGHT NOW,
MY HEART IS RACING LIKE IT WAS THAT DAY.

NOW
I REALLY BELIEVE THAT
TUMBLE
ポロ...
MAYBE NOT RIGHT THIS SECOND,
BUT I DO WANT TO TALK TO FUJI AGAIN.
Aaw...
What is with her ...?
BADUM BADUM BADUM
ドキ ドキドキ
She grabbed my hand out of nowhere!
She even got me to squeeze back!!
VROOM
ブォン
AAHH!
BAKRAK
AAAAA AAAAA AAGH!!
part 2 ♥ END

M o t e k i   M i t s u r o u   K u b o

M o t e k i

M i t s u r o u K u b o

Motekis That Might Be Amazing ①

A SPIN-OFF STARRING SUMI: "MOTEKI NEXT LEVEL ~THEY ARE ALL MY LOVERS~"
Starring
Sumida
Fuck Buddy, Itsuka Naka-shiba
Ex-Fiancée, Natsuki Komi-yama
Daugh-ter, Yuma Haya-shida
Ex-Wife and Bar Manager, Naoko Haya-shida
Lover/ Secretary, Aki Doi
How did all this happen without my knowing ...?
This isn't what a *moteki* is, right ...? Right ?!

Motekis That Might Be Amazing ②

MANY MONTHS LATER ...
I'm home ...
IN THE END,
Wel- come home, "Dad- dy!" ♡
I MARRIED YUMI, WHO I MET JUST BY CHANCE.
You've never called me "Daddy" be- fore, right? Isn't it a bit too soon?
AH HA HA HA HA HA HA
HEH HEH HEH HEH
Well, you'll be a daddy next year!

I'M GLAD IT WORKED OUT THIS WAY.

TRUE HAPPINESS IS SOMETHING THAT SHOWS UP RIGHT BY YOUR SIDE. I SHOULD NEVER HAVE GOTTEN SO CAUGHT UP IN SOMETHING LIKE A *MOTEKI*...

INCOMING CALL

What ... a call ?

At this hour ...?

I'M HAVING MY *MOTEKI*... AGAIN!!!!

What?! A 2nd *moteki* ?!

PFFT

Aren't there already a ton of stories like this?

Well, it's a world I know nothing about...

If I wrote this, people would say, "Mitsuro isn't even married. This sort of thing is beyond her, which makes it hilarious," right?

ABOUT **MITSUROU KUBO**

Mitsurou Kubo is a manga artist born in Nagasaki prefecture. Her series *3.3.7 Byoshi!!* (2001-2003), *Tokkyu!!* (2004-2008), and *Again!!* (2011-2014) were published in *Weekly Shonen Magazine*, and *Moteki* (2008-2010) was published in the seinen comics magazine *Evening*. After the publication of *Again!!* concluded, she met Sayo Yamamoto, director of the global smash-hit anime ***Yuri!!! on ICE***. Working with Yamamoto, Kubo contributed the original concept, original character designs, and initial script for ***Yuri!!! on ICE***. *Again!!* is her first manga to be published in English.

MOTEKI Love Strikes! 2

Translation: Ko Ransom
Production: Risa Cho
Eve Grandt

First published in Japan in 2010 by Kodansha, Ltd., Tokyo
Publication for this English edition arranged through Kodansha, Ltd., Tokyo
English language version produced by Vertical, Inc.

Translation provided by Vertical, Inc., 2018
Published by Vertical Comics, an imprint of Vertical, Inc., New York

Originally published in Japanese as *Moteki 3 - 4.5* by Kodansha, Ltd., 2010
Moteki first serialized in *Evening*, Kodansha, Ltd., 2008 - 2010
This is a work of fiction.

ISBN: 978-1-945054-81-5

Manufactured in Canada

First Edition

Vertical, Inc.
451 Park Avenue South
7th Floor
New York, NY 10016
www.vertical-comics.com

Vertical books are distributed through Pengiun-Random House Publisher Services.